SATAN WAS
A LESBIAN

Satan Was A Lesbian
by Fred Haley

Originally published 1966

New Edition Published by Pulp Culture Press
44 Race Street
San Jose, CA 95126

www.pulpculturepress.com

ISBN: 978-1-59362-318-0

PULPCULTURE
press

SATAN WAS A LESBIAN

FRED HALEY

For all the people who ever said to me "My Girlfriend needs this book!"

Editors Notes

Imagine a conversation that went something like this:

Editor: Hey Fred, gimmie 50,000 words about a lesbian who turns out to be the devil!

Fred: Uh, sure

Editor, Do you know any lesbians or gay people?

Fred: No.

Editor: Perfect, I need it next week, here is the cover art to get the juices flowing.

Satan Was A Lesbian is something of a minor pop-culture phenomena. Images of the cover appear on t-shirts, zippo lighters, posters, prints, beach towels and on and on and on. All of these things are inspired by the title which is catchy and inspires everything from mild giggles to outright exasperated laughter. I know because we sell some of these things and I hear people go "pfff... Satan Was A Lesbian, my girlfriend *so* needs this".

After a while I became curious about the book and finally managed to get my hands on it. I sat down to read it hoping I would find some sort of forgotten gem or some other outdated story that is funny now in retrospect.

Nope, not even close.

The only thing I discovered is that this book is bad. Maybe not the worst thing I have ever read, but just bad. What we have here is obviously something that was a product of its time where the editor wanted lesbian sleaze because it sold and the writer wanted a gig that paid. Writers are like musicians in that they think that the next job they get is going to be the last one they ever get offered so of course this one took the job.

The things I gleaned from reading Satan Was A Lesbian were:

a) The author had probably never met a lesbian.

b) They were getting paid by the word or page, and there was a limit to the number of words or pages.

c) Satan has nothing to do with this and does not appear in the book

I decided to republish this book in a new edition since given its pop-culture significance it deserves to be available if for no other reasons as a historical reference. Some people will find this book a little triggering as there is a fair amount of violence in it. There is also a scene with some kittens that I wanted to exclude however it gets referenced a few times in the rest of the book, so in it stayed.

What I did for this edition was clean up some of the typos, set it in a more readable format, added some chapter names (the original only had numbers), and in a few places changed some wording so that the text was not as repetitive. I also added graphics to the start of each chapter so that you might feel you got some added value for buying this book.

I was tempted to re-write the entire book in order to make it funnier or sexier or something, but I think the story was better left unchanged. However somewhere on my hard drive there exists the start of a short story that takes the theme of Satan being a Lesbian and tries to make something funny out of it.

Who knows, if I published that it could wind up being a best-seller.

Dan Vado
Edition Editor

TABLE OF CONTENTS

1

CALL HER CHARLEY

The dark Impala slashed recklessly through the rain swept streets, buffeted by violent gusts of wind, battered by the solid sheets of water raking it. It slued around comers, tires slipping dangerously on the flooded streets, sometimes nearly reversing its direction of travel. Behind the wheel, sitting easily but erect, Charlene Duval directed the charge with assured touch, a faint smile on her lips as she glanced from time to time at the taut figure of the girl beside her, who was staring with hypnotized eyes through the partially clouded windshield. Her smile widened imperceptibly each time the sound of a muffled gasp reached her ears, each time a small hand let go its death-grip on the edge of the seat to be caught between the white teeth of the terrified blonde.

The ride had started conventionally enough, with the petite blonde leaning loosely against the door on her side of the car, her face turned toward Charlene, one foot drawn up under her, a happy smile on her face. There had been light chatter and laughter. Then Charlene had begun to put more and more weight on the accelerator, and the other girl had straightened, both feet on the floor, face forward, her smile giving way to a look of tension. "Charlene ... " No answer, but the speed increased again. The blonde's hands became little fists and she scooted an inch closer to the driver's side of the car. "Charlene ... " Again the speed crept upward, and again the blonde scooted closer, eyes wide, breathing rate keeping pace with the acceleration of the car. This had gone on from increase to increase, until now the blonde was plastered tightly against Charlene's side. One hand gripping Charlene's knee with all her strength, her breathing so heavy and gasping that it almost drowned out the sound of the rain, wind, and motor combined.

Charlene's thin smile widened again, her foot came down on the accelerator, her eyes flicked to the blonde, noting the shining lips, loosely moving, the tongue coming out to wet them even more. Charlene's eyes dropped to the bulging breasts under the coat sweater, and noted that the nipples protruded nakedly, even under the woven material. She could almost feel the hardness of them. Her eyes returned to the street, and her foot put the last ounce of pressure on the accelerator with a sudden lunge the car lept.

"*CHARLENE* . . . " The word was a shriek, echoing about the tightly closed car. The hand on Charlene's knee moved convulsively, raking her thigh, the blonde head buried itself in her shoulder, and now she could feel the sobbing of the girl's breathing. She chuckled softly, took her foot off the accelerator and let the car slow of its own accord. She took another sluing tum, felt the blonde's arms go about her and the burning face bury itself in her throat. She shook her head and craned her neck to see over the blonde mop, swung the car into the curb and braked lightly to a stop under the dripping leaves of a huge tree.

She sat quietly, hands still on the wheel, feeling the soft lips on her throat, the burning of the girl's breath, the trembling arms and hands clasping her in tight embrace. Her eyes moved over what she could see through the steamed-up windows and windshield. Black, dripping landscape. Houses standing back from the street, silent, dark, seemingly deserted. Ahead, casting only a ghostly glow into the car because of distance and rain, a solitary street light. A black, glistening world, out of a dark dream, and the black, short-cropped hair and the black eyes of Charlene Duval were in perfect keeping with it, as were the black thoughts that moved behind the finely sculptured features of the haunting face.

Now little flecks of reflected light bounced from the bottomless black irises as if in frustration at their inability to penetrate the wall before them as the eyes turned downward toward the top of the blonde head nestled under her chin, the lips constantly moving against her throat. Charlene smiled again, a secretive smile, slipped an arm around the waist of her partner, tilted the girl's head up with her free hand. "Darling, my shoulders feel a little tight. Do you suppose you could-"

"Oh yes, Charlene. I'd love to."

"Thank you, darling." Charlene turned in the seat, presented her back to the other girl. She closed her eyes as she felt the tiny hands close over the muscles of her shoulders and begin a gentle massaging.

"Um.mm, that's nice."
"I like to feel you under my hands, Charlene."
"Have you forgotten my name already, darling?"
"No, Charlene. I - I mean, Charley." The moving hands tightened a little. "That's such a lovely name. Charley. I love it. I - I love you, Charley."

"Ummm."

"_But - but, Charley, you have such a strange way; you frighten me. I just can't understand you at all, what makes you do such things?" The hands had tightened again and begun to move faster as the blonde mentioned the frightening, and Charlene moved sensuously under their touch. "That's it, darling. That's it. You want to know why I'm me, is that it? Well, I don't know. But you wouldn't want it any different, would you?"

The blonde drew a deep breath and buried her lips in the side of Charlene's neck. "No, darling, I guess not." She rolled her face deeper into the curve of the slender neck. "Oh God, when you frighten me ..."

Charlene squirmed again. "I know, darling, I know. Wonderful, isn't it." She tilted her head to one side, to allow the seeking lips more freedom in their wandering over her neck.
"You know it is, you - you she-devil." The girl sobbed once, and

her teeth closed on the firm column of Charlene's throat. "Oh God, darling, it's hellish and it's wonderful!" Then her tongue-tip was trying to remove the teeth-marks left by her spasmodic nip and her lips were sliding damply over the white expanse beneath them.

Charlene sighed contentedly, murmured, "You're forgetting your job, baby."
"I'm sorry, Charley, but - " and her voice dropped to a low whisper - "I can't remember anything when - " She bit her lip, returning to her rubbing of Charlene's shoulders. Then she caught her breath with a gasp as Charlene's right hand came up to undo the top button of the white blouse. "Now you can work a little more effectively, sweetheart."

"Y-yes, Charley." The girl's hands tremblingly spread the blouse collar back as far as the next button would allow and put her hands on the naked flesh of Charlene's shoulders. Her eyes tried to see over one white shoulder and down into the depths of the well-filled blouse, but she relaxed in disappointment. Charlene sensed her chagrin, chuckled softly and loosened another button. • "Don't be impatient, darling. Anything worthwhile takes time, to coin a phrase."

She moved again, lazily and sensuously, as the eager fingers spread the blouse collar a little further. She reached up and drew the girl's hands to the front of her shoulders, pressing them into the hollow below her collar-bones. "I'm tight in front too, darling." Her grip on the girl's wrists firmed. "But easy, baby. Everything in its own time." She laughed softly. "Tonight's my night for old saws."

The hands were moving again, there was silence, and then Charlene loosened a third button. Again the blouse gaped wide open and the hands slipped lower. Another button, and now the avid fingers were sinking into the tops of swelling breasts, gleaming softly in the dim light. The petite blonde had slid back gradually, and Charlene was now half-lying back against the front of her body. Charlene had noted the gradual change of position, but had ignored it, chuckling to herself at the girl's attempted cleverness.

She rose slightly. "Slide back, darling, so I can... stretch out."

"Y-yes, Charley. Yes." The blonde scooted back against the door and her hands helped Charlene to lie back, the dark head cradled in the other girl's lap. Charlene drew a deep breath, looking up into the white face over her, watching the wide eyes fix on the upward movement of the half-covered breasts beneath the white blouse. "Easy, darling. Take it easy." She reached up and undid another button.

The blonde's hands were trembling uncontrollably now, but they were very slow and deliberate in spreading the blouse a bit more, revealing the shadowed crevice between the upward-pointing hills. Then the hands were moving on the softness, slipping into the valley, gently squeezing. The wide eyes and the trembling fingers were still baffled in their seeking of the yearned for nipples, and the girl's breathing was now almost a continuous sobbing sound. Her fingers brushed the edge of the tight brassiere, and she uttered a tiny sound, then a louder sob.

"Oh God, Charley. Don't! Don't do this to me! Please, darling, please!" A tear ran down her cheek and splashed on Charlene's forehead. And Charlene finally relented. Her hand came up_ and loosened the last button. "All right, darling. But remember, slow and easy." With a little whine the blonde spread the blouse wide open, then, supporting Charlene's upper body with one hand, worked the blouse down over her arms, her hands running in light, hungry caresses the length of the firm, bare, round arms. She whispered endless caressing sounds of adoration, and Charlene, eyes closed, smiled dreamily. She felt the restrained urge for speed in the tiny fingers as they slipped around to search for the clasp of her brassiere. She arched her back to assist in the seeking, then slumped again as she felt the bouncing lift of her freed breasts. Now Charlene's head was lying on the seat, and the palpitating blonde was sliding to her knees on the floor of the car, hands inching upward from Charlene's slender, naked waist toward the sharp rise still covered by the loose bra.

"Easy, darling. Take the bra clear off first."

"Yes, Charley, yes." The hands reluctantly left her smooth skin, lifted the bra delicately and began slipping it down her arms. Charlene smiled her dreamy smile again as the hands found it absolutely impossible to resist brushing the upthrust of her firm-skinned breasts in their work. Her slitted eyes watched the other's wide gaze fix and remain on her nipples, feeling the nipples hardening under the hot scrutiny.

Then the bra was gone and the hands were moving slowly, ever so slowly, over the smoothness of her shoulders, then curling around the base of her breasts, slipping up and up toward the peaks. At the same time, the girl's face was sinking closer, just as slowly. And finally the hands tightened and the open mouth settled slowly, softly, and moistly over one rigid crest.

The mouth moved faster, tongue flicking. Sounds of muffled, heavy breathing increased. Charlene turned her face toward the body bent over her, slipped her arm around the svelte waist and drew the body closer, burying her face between the sweater covered breasts. Her hand moved up under the back of the sweater, running over the sleek back, unmarred by brassiere band. Her mouth moved in a smile against the bulging sweater. Her little slave had come well prepared. Her hand edged around to the girl's side in a sliding caress, moving upward to cup itself around one bare, throbbing breast. The girl's body moved back slightly to give her more room, and her hand slipped across to repeat its inspection of the other pendent delight.

The girl's mouth was wild and urning now, and Charlene's smile was constant. Her hand eased down to the bottom button of the sweater, then to the next one up, her lips stroking each inch of flesh as it was exposed. The body was trembling violently now, and Charlene wondered how long it would be before the labored breathing could be heard outside the car, assuming anyone was silly enough to be out there on a night like this. She uttered a little croon of contentment, loosened another button, pressed another kiss. She reached the last button, the sweater swung open, and the quivering nipples were waiting for her lips. She slid her arm around the slim waist again, her hand flat on the girl's upper back.

No pull was needed. The plump breasts swung of their own

accord against her face. Her mouth kissed, her tongue laved. The heartbeat behind the softness was drum-like, off time in an erratic beat. And when her mouth captured a resilient nipple, a muffled cry came from the mouth so eagerly worshiping her own breasts.

Outside the car, the wind increased in violence, the rain became a solid torrent. Inside, the windows fogged more. Outside, it was getting colder. Inside, the temperature seemed to go up and up. Despite this fact, however, Charlene's lips finally abandoned their delicious feast and her hands tugged the blonde head up to press the girl's flushed cheek to her lips. "I'm chilly, darling."

The small blonde looked down at her, then at her own open sweater. She smiled slowly, took the edges of the sweater in her hands and spread it like a pair of wings. She turned her body to one side, rose up over Charlene and lowered her upper body down over that of her lover, her lower body half-on, half-off the seat, one thigh nestled tightly against Charlene's, one knee still on the floor of the car. Charlene watched her impassively, her black eyes going to the pendant breasts as they slowly flattened against her own, her stomach relishing the pressure of the other's as it moved sinuously to fit their curves and hollows snugly together.

The girl's warm arms closed around Charlene, cuddling them both in the folds of the sweater. Her lips came down on Charlene's, teasing them, slid to her cheek, then buried themselves in the side of Charlene's neck, her face snuggled tightly into Charlene's warmth. After a moment her lips began to move again, over Charlene's forehead, her closed eyes, her cheeks, her lips. They nestled against Charlene's ear, whispering softly, "I'd never let you get cold, Charley darling. I'd never let anything bad happen to you. I love you too much."

"That's my sweet Cynthia." Charlene's lips touched the girl's bare shoulder, then her hands urged the other's lips to her own. Her tongue moved slowly between Cynthia's lips, then faster as the other hungry tongue moved to meet it. Again the temperature seemed to rise, as nipples tightened against each other, and the activity sped up – upward and back. She sat up, sliding her hands lightly to cover Cynthia's breasts. "Let me turn around, darling," she whispered. Her hands remained still, savoring the quivering swing of Cynthia's breasts as the girl moved back to allow her to bring her feet around so that she was again sitting behind the steering wheel of the car, her legs stretched out indolently toward Cynthia, her hands releasing their light grip on the girl's flesh. "My slacks seem to be binding me, darling. Everything feels too tight on me."

Cynthia's eyes gleamed. "Yes, Charley. I - I'll fix it." Her hands went to the zipper of Charlene's uniform slacks, lowered it quickly. Then they tugged the slacks down, taking the top of her panties along, moving ever faster as they freed Charlene's knees from the covering "binding" them. They released the slacks and panties, and moved down to tear off the flat shoes and heavy socks covering her feet. Then the hands returned to strip slacks and panties off and, picking up everything, tossed it into the back of the car.

As she looked up again, her eyes sweeping the nude white body stretched out before her, Cynthia heard another whisper. "My feet ache, darling." The black eyes were fixed unblinkingly on her face. She tore her gaze away with an effort and picked up one slender foot, rubbing it between her hands, her fingers tightening and loosening, feeling the fine bones. Her eyes watched the toes flex and curl, and then her mouth was kissing that foot, loving each toe, moving up to caress the ankle, then the calf. She laid the foot on the seat of the car, huddled over it, hands stroking, lips sliding. She felt Charlene's other foot moving, slipping under her open sweater, along her waist, felt it wiggling against her breast, trying to grip her nipple between the first and second toes. And she heard another whisper. "Aren't you too warm in all those clothes, darling?"

She looked up again, completely unaware of the inconsistency of the question in the light of Charlene's complaint of a few minutes earlier about being chilly. "Y -yes. Charley." Charlene gave her another lazy smile.

"Well . . . " Cynthia bent and pressed a last quick kiss on the calf of Charlene's leg, straightened, her hands flying to the edges of her sweater, but a sharply whispered "No" brought her to a sudden dead halt, her wide eyes fixed on Charlene's lips. Those lips were tight, but they slowly relaxed in that dreamy smile that Cynthia was becoming so accustomed to — and so fond of. The lips moved. "Darling, no, not so fast. We have all the time in the world. The whole night, if we want it, in our own cozy little world. Just the two of us, with no one to see, hear, or say anything. Slowly, darling, slowly. Do it in slow motion, and keep your eyes on mine while you do it. I want your eyes to talk to mine, baby. I want them to tell me how you feel, how much you want me." Again came the lazy smile. "You do want me, don't you, sweetheart?"

"Oh God, Charley, I can't tell you how much. Please, please don't torture me like this. I'm dying for you, and you keep me hanging back, driving myself crazy. Please, darling . . . "

Charlene completely ignored the plea. "Let your eyes tell me how much, baby. Let your every slow, slow movement tell me. She paused. Then: "All right, darling. Start. Very, very slowly now." Cynthia's body straightened, still kneeling at Charlene's feet, and her hands began as slowly and gracefully as they could, considering their tremulous state, to remove the sweater. She was extremely conscious of the protuberant condition of her bare breasts as her arms went back to allow the sweater to come off over her hands. She was even more conscious of the black, fathomless eyes fixed on them, watching their every shiver and swing. The ache in them increased as the unblinking eyes watched. Eventually the sweater was gone, and she opened the zipper of her skirt. Small though she was, she was crowded, crouched there on the floor, and she had to half stand awkwardly under the low top of the car, twisting and turning to get rid of the skirt, then the panties, shoes, and stockings. Not daring to remove her eyes from Charlene's made it doubly difficult.

She felt her breasts swinging loosely with her movements, and they seemed to double in weight as those hellish, wonderful, heavenly eyes watched, the face weirdly beautiful and unchanging in the slightest degree of expression. Cynthia couldn't stand the silence any longer. "Charlene ... uh ... Charley, please, please say something. You frighten me. You look - dead."

No response of any kind. "Charley, please!" Her voice was a thin shriek, and her hands came up to cover and clasp her breasts, which had taken on an unbearable feeling of tightness and pain. Her eyes pleaded for some sign of movement, change of expression. And she almost sobbed with relief as the shadowy lips moved the slightest bit, issuing a ghostly summons. "The gates of Hell are waiting, Cynthia. Enter, and be eternally damned."

Cynthia was shaken to her heels by the intensity and content of the words, and her feeling of relief was forgotten. Then she giggled almost hysterically. "God, Charley, if you scare me any more I'll go out of my mind. So help me, I will!"

The evil, beloved lips smiled openly this time, and the whisper was heated. "Come on, darling, come on, before we both go out of our minds." Cynthia jumped as she suddenly felt a foot on either side of her, the toes moving over her ribs in that strange caress that made her feel so wonderfully and completely subjugated. She reached down, smoothing the flesh on the calves of Charlene's legs. She lowered her head, bending low at the waist, to kiss first one then the other of those calves, feeling as if she were bowing to an idol. And she was. Oh yes, Charley was idol enough for anyone, and she felt indescribably wonderful and thrilled to be allowed to humiliate herself before her goddess. Her lips moved to the knees, her head swinging from one side to the other so as not to neglect either. She kissed the soft flesh just above each knee, then went on, and on.

Charlene accepted this homage without any kind of movement except for her hands, which crept down to stroke the blonde hair of her worshiper, to skim caressingly over the soft, warm shoulders, to ruffle the hair on the back of Cynthia's neck.

Then a quick, sharp sigh escaped her and her body surged upward, settled back slowly. Her black eyes watched the top of the blonde head, watched her own fingers moving over the fine hair, and her lips softened. Slowly her eyes closed, and she felt her body beginning to move involuntarily under the unceasing assault of the warm lips of her abject slave. Oh, it was nice. So very nice. And so very, very easy to accomplish. It was nearly impossible to believe that she had met this wonderful plaything only last night. But it was easy. All you had to do was find the right trigger, and then press it. Everyone, everything had one trigger that would release anything you wanted. Just find it. Charlene sighed again, twitched, tightened her hands on the blonde head. Only last night ...

• • •

It had been raining last night, but not quite so hard as it was now, and business at Hal's drive-in had been dead. Charlene had been in one of her bad moods, and sitting around with nothing to do hadn't helped at all. A glance at the clock showed her that she had one more hour to go. Two in the morning, she was think-ing, was one hell of a time for anyone to be going home from work. She had reached the point of thinking that anything was a hell of a thing for anyone to be doing, when she saw the wet, dark car pull into one of the stalls of her station. "Some no-tip-ping big wheel from nowhere," she groused, and took her time about getting out to see what he wanted.

When she first looked through the water-streaked, steam-cloud-ed window she was startled for a moment. She thought she was looking into the eyes of a child behind the wheel. But as the win-dow came down, and she hunched her raincoat-clad shoulders over as much of the opening as she could, she realized that it was neither a he nor a child. It was a diminutive girl, whose face she had a vague feeling she'd seen before.

"Hi, Charlene." The tiny blonde was smiling uncertainly, her eyes fixed on Charlene's.

Charlene gave no outward sign of surprise at the girl's knowl-edge of her name. "Hello there." Then she asked unblinking-ly, "How do you know me, and who are you?" The girl's smile became even more uncertain. "Oh, one of the other girls told me - and I'm Cynthia Loomis."

Charlene looked her over, wondering how her feet ever reached the accelerator and brake, then as her eyes caught the swell of magnificent breasts distorting the front of a button-front sweater, she wondered with an inner smile what the penalty might be for violating the law of gravity as this chick was doing. Unless, of course, the gal wore a bra with knots in the centers of the cups.

Her eyes remained fixed on those forward looking beauties, until the girl squirmed uneasily. Nope, Charlene decided, watching the unfettered movement under the sweater. No bra.
"What - what are you looking at, Charlene? Have I got dirt somewhere?"

"No, Cynthia. I was watching your breasts, to see if you had on a bra."

Cynthia blinked, then again, and her mouth opened. Then she laughed, still uncertainly. "You - you're very frank, aren't you!"

"Why not?"

Again the shaky laugh. "Yes, why not?" "What would you like, Cynthia?" The girl looked flustered. "Why, I - I don't know." Charlene groaned aloud. "For God's sake don't tell me you want to ruin a menu, plus good food, by trying to read or eat in this atmosphere. Look, there's a restaurant not far from here, where you can - "

"No, please, Charlene. I'm not particularly hungry. Could you just bring me a cup of coffee?" Her eyes were staring into Charlene's, a little puzzled frown wrinkling the smoothness between her eyes. "Your eyes are completely black, aren't they?"

Charlene restrained a bored smile. "Yes, Cynthia, completely black." How many times had she heard that question, she wondered. "Coffee coming up. You won't need a tray for that, will you?"

"Oh no, I'll just set it up here." Cynthia's hand waved vaguely at the area of the windshield, her eyes still watching Charlene's face. Then, as Charlene moved toward the service window, Cynthia called to her. "Bring two, Charlene, will you?"

Charlene waved assent, got the two cups together with cream and sugar, and returned to the car. Cynthia rolled the window down again and took the cups. "One's for you, Charlene. Could - could you sit in the car and drink it with me?"

The black eyes studied her in silence, then swung around the empty lot to the lethargic counterman inside, came back to Cynthia. Her lips asked the question that answered so many questions. "Why not?" She walked around the car, opened the door slightly, whipped off her dripping raincoat and tossed it over the fender of the car, jumped inside quickly and slammed the door. Cynthia had rolled up the window, and now the air was still and cozy. Charlene picked up one of the cups, disdained the cream and sugar, looked at Cynthia, and said, "Well?"

Cynthia blinked again. She was to blink often in her relationship with Charlene. "Well what?" "Well, here I am. Now what?" "N-nothing ... I just wanted to talk with you." "About what?" "Why - why nothing in particular. Just... talk."

"So talk."

"But - but, my God, Charlene, you sound as if you expected me to accuse you of something." Charlene smiled a little. "Okay, honey, I'm sorry. But when people go out of their way to talk to me they usually want something. Have I got something you want?"

Cynthia's hands twisted in her lap."N-no. I just want to talk with you."

"So we're right back where we started. Talk."

Cynthia gave a hopeless, helpless light laugh. "You don't make it easy, Charlene."

"Nothing's easy, honey. But nothing."

Cynthia's voice warmed."That's one of the things I wanted to talk with you about. You've got a . . . a... fateful look about you, as if you'd looked into the depths of hell, and still remember vividly what you saw there. You've got a look of tragedy about you, Charlene."

Charlene groaned for the second time at this girl. "Oh Christ, a spy-novel reader. An amateur dramatist. Or are you one of those home-grown headshrinkers who've got the answers to all the world's problems at their fingertips, if you'll excuse the neologism."

Cynthia looked down at her hands. "Laugh if you want to. I - I've watched you. You probably don't remember even seeing me, but I've watched you a couple of times, for quite a while each time. You've got a depth about you. You're a lot more than appears on the surface - unless someone watches that surface for a long time. It breaks through every once in a while. You fascinate me, Charlene. You'll laugh again to hear it, but you've got a scent of hell about you." Cynthia paused for a moment, then asked abruptly. "Are you married?"

Again the black eyes settled on hers in silence. "No. Never have been, and don't plan to be." The blank gaze held her eyes until Cynthia blushed, squirmed, tried to drop her eyes, but couldn't manage it. Finally she murmured, "Please, Charlene. . . "

Charlene was suddenly smiling, her voice more animated. "Go ahead, honey, You talk and I'll talk. You ask and I'll answer. We'll see if we can't clarify the old mystery. You're the only one who knows what mystery is, so you'll have to lead."

Then the black eyes were fixed again on Cynthia's face, motionless. Cynthia blushed again, "Oh, I don't know what's the matter with me. Maybe you're right. Maybe I'm just an amateur dramatist - who doesn't know how to write."

"Don't worry about it, honey. Everybody has his quirks, as the saying goes. Who knows what's wrong with whom? The whole world is probably nuts, including both of us."

Cynthia regained a semblance of a smile. "Or one of us. I wonder which one. Most probably me. I know that - " She caught the black eyes on her again, and blushed a deep red.

"What do you know, Cynthia? You got secrets too? Come on. Maybe we can cure each other of our ills." The tone was mocking, and Cynthia couldn't miss it, but she took the words at their face value.

"Yes, of course, Charlene. I guess everybody has secrets. I guess - oh hell, I'm talking like a flaming romance• magazine." She dropped her eyes again to the twisting hands in her lap. A dim light began to glow in the back of Charlene's mind. Her eyes moved down to the girl's prominent breasts. Yep, those knots were still there. Well, it wasn't all that chilly in the car, what with the heater on low speed and all the windows closed. And nipples don't normally ... Charlene smiled her slow smile, reached out a hand and patted the girl on a soft shoulder. "It's okay, honey. Life's a flaming romance magazine from start to finish. Why shouldn't you talk like one if you feel like it?"

Cynthia looked at her again, a little sheepishly. "Thanks, Charlene. You're very kind."
Charlene snorted. "Kind, hell. I'm nuts, remember? I've got a scent of hell about me." She sniffed, audibly. "Hmmm. Does seem to be a touch of brimstone in the air. Oh well. And you're the li'l ol' gal who's gonna cure that. Or have you forgotten pore li'l ol' me already?" She rubbed one arm under her nose, sniffling heart-brokenly, then rubbed the arm along her pants leg, inspected it closely, and rubbed it again against her slacks.
"Please, Charlene. Talk about corny ... talk about flaming romances . . . " Suddenly she cut off the laugh, and looked quickly about the lot. "Charlene, I've got an idea." She caught Charlene's hand. "Could you get away from this place? Take a ride with me? You've only got a little - " She stopped short, blushed again, deeply.

Charlene laughed softly. "Really checked up on me, haven't you, doll?"

Cynthia looked almost panic-stricken. "No, no, Charlene. I - I only asked . . . " She slowed to a stop, looking completely miserable. "I know, honey, I know. You found out I get off at two. Well, I'm flattered that you even wondered." "Are you, really?" Cynthia's tone was half-shamed, half-eager.

"Sure, honey. How many people give enough of a damn about other people to care when they get off work - or when they drop dead, for that matter?"

"Then -then you don't mind? You don't think-" "Honey, I don't think nothin' except that you're a real tiny, sweet doll who's got a great big heart." With another glance at the girl's·breasts, she added a few words, but silently, to herself.

Cynthia's smile thanked her. "Well, do you think-" Again came the sure answer. "Why not?"

Charlene slipped out of the car, grabbed her raincoat and threw it about her shoulders, ran to the service window, where she informed the counterman that she was leaving, right now. The man glanced at the clock, back at her, opened his mouth to protest.

"Sue me," Charlene shot over her shoulder on the way back to the car. She was so intent on her own thoughts that she didn't even think about her bag, lying under the counter inside. Positive action, that was the answer. Get in the first and last word. Leave 'em with their mouths open. To hell with 'em.

Inside the car, she dropped her raincoat on the floor between her feet. "So go, honey. Drive."

"W-where to, Charlene?"

"Who the hell cares? Just go." "Do you have a car here?" "Sure. So what about it? I sure as hell can't ride with you and drive it too."

"No, of course not. Well, as you say, to hell with it!" Cynthia seemed caught in the mood that Charlene projected. To hell with everyone and everything. Just go, go, go.

As they got underway, Charlene threw her arm over the back of the seat and relaxed. ·'Where do you live, honey?"
"Kanesville," Cynthia answered. Then her face lit up. "Would you

like to go there, Charlene? My folks are gone for a few days, and we could relax over drinks and talk. Would you like that, Charlene?"

Charlene smiled one of her lazy smiles. "I'd love it, baby. Good booze, I hope."

"Oh yes, my father drinks only the best of - " She broke off, frowned at Charlene. "You're laughing at me."

"No, no, baby. I just like good booze." Her eyes were on the swell of Cynthia's breasts. Were those knots just the least bit more obvious? After a short silence Charlene said casually, "Honey, you said a little while ago that you were probably the one of us who's nuts. You added something like "I know that - " and then you blushed like crazy. What do you know that's all that upsetting?"

Cynthia looked over at her, but Charlene casually leaned back against the seat, her eyes closed. "Oh, it's nothing, really. It's just that I frighten ridiculously easily, and . . . and . . . "

"And what, honey?"

"Nothing, Charlene. I'd rather not talk about it." Charlene looked at her, caught her glance and leered. "Okay, baby. I'll get you loaded good and proper on your own booze, and then you'll tell me." She dry-washed her hands and leered again melodramatically. "I'll learn all your innermost secrets, me proud beauty. And then you'll be in me *powah. Heh heh heh.*"

Cynthia laughed nervously. "Charlene, you're trying to be corny, but you sound like the devil himself."

"I am, honey, I am. Just call me Lucifer." Her eyes fell once more on Cynthia's bulging breasts and vivid pictures came into her mind. "Yep, honey, I'm the Old Man himself." Cynthia's answer was almost a whisper. "I almost believe you, Charlene, I really do."

"How much further, honey?"

"We're almost there. It's only about seven miles from my house to the drive-in."

"Well, hurry, baby. My throat's gettin' mighty dry!' Charlene clutched her throat, husked, "Whiskey, whiskey! Ah ben in thet thar desert fer three days, an' ah'm dyin'! *Whiskey!*"

She watched Cynthia's face out of the corner of her eye during this delivery, and was relieved to see the laugh form, chasing the slight frown that had been there. Com still had its uses. She decided to be a little more circumspect in her remarks for a while.

When they finally pulled into the driveway beside an old fashioned two-story house, Charlene was surprised to see the place ablaze with light. "Is this it, honey?" At Cynthia's "yes" Charlene added: "But I thought you said there was nobody home."

"There isn't. I - I just like a lot of light, and I don't like to come home to a dark house."

"Oh, yeah. You scare easily. But how come you stay home alone if you're all that jittery?"

"It's not that I'm afraid of any specific thing, like burglars or something like that. It's just - just that I never know what's going to scare me. If I leave the lights on I feel a lot better."
They were halfway from the street to the side of the house when the rain took a sudden notion to let everything go at once. By the time Cynthia had stopped the car the visibility was nearly zero. They sat and stared wordlessly out of the windows for a moment - Then Cynthia picked out a key in her case and held it separate from the rest. "Come on, Charlene. You've got a raincoat, and we can run like mad." She held up the key. "It'll only take a second to get inside."

Charlene shrugged, picked up her raincoat and threw it around her shoulders. "Lead on, Captain." She threw open her door and jumped out, followed by Cynthia, who had scooted across the seat to use the same door rather th,n run around the car in the driving flood. They ran for the house - and Cynthia dropped the key ring. She let out a wail and started looking frantically for it, scrabbling in the grass along the path. By the time she found it she was soaked to the skin, despite Charlene's attempt to cover them both with the raincoat.

Inside the house, They looked at each other and laughed. "Cynthia honey, you look like you'd been in the river for a week." "You don't look too dry yourself. How's the swimming?" Then Cynthia was busy being the gracious hostess. She grabbed Charlene's hand, tugged. "Come on up the stairs. We'll get out of these wet clothes - - and into a dry martini! *Heh heh heh.*" Cynthia giggled, dragging Charlene to the stairway. "Yes, we'll do that too."

Charlene pretended to be shocked. "My Gawd, gal, a martini after dinner?" Cynthia tugged impatiently at her hand. "Well, there's almost anything else you want. Come on, idiot. Don't argue with me." She looked up from her five foot height to Charlene's five-feet-eight. "I'll turn you over my knee if you don't watch out."
"
Okay, Maw, I'll be good."

Upstairs, Cynthia dragged her into a comfortably furnished bedroom with an old fashioned double bed. "My parents' bedroom." She opened a closet, brought out a wooly robe. "My mother's about the same size as me, but my father's robe shouldn't be much too big for you." She giggled again. "You'd wreck one of mine, and besides, you'd look silly in it."

Charlene studied the robe for a moment, then stroked her chin thoughtfully. "Well, ah reckon ah could be yore ol' man fer a while, at that." She looked at Cynthia severely. "And we'll have no more talk about yore venerable ol' pa lookin' silly under any conditions."

"Yes - I mean no, Daddy." Cynthia sobered. "Hey, maybe you want a shower after working most of the night."

"Well, I could use a shower, but I did damn little work tonight."

Cynthia was tugging at her hand again. "Right in here, Charlene. The house may be old fashioned in looks, but it's got modern plumbing. You go ahead, while I go to my room and try to remedy the damage." Charlene held back. "Look, you're in worse shape than I am. You go ahead and take your shower first, I can wait."

Cynthia grinned up at her, then adopted the air of a Grande Dame, looking down her nose at Charlene. This was a ludicrous sight, as she had to bend her head so far back as nearly to break her neck in order to accomplish the feat. "I, my dear young woman, have my own shower, which I used just before coming down to see the peasant life at the drive-in." She dropped the pose and rubbed the back of her neck. "Now go to it, gal. I'll see you in a few minutes."

When Charlene finished her operations in the bathroom, she came out to find Cynthia sprawled on the bed, wearing a high-necked full-length housecoat, quilted and very demure. But even the modest garment couldn't hide the thrust of the spectacular bosom beneath it. Charlene wondered if the knots were still evident on that bosom. The housecoat did hide that. The man's robe was just a little too long in the sleeves, and Charlene was absorbed in turning the cuff's back when she heard Cynthia giggle again. "Why, Daddy, you've lost weight, I do believe. At least through the middle." She cocked her head to one side. "But you seem to have gained a little upstairs and downstairs."

Charlene smiled her faint smile, and when her answer came in the deepest voice she could muster, Cynthia's eyes popped. "Well, my dear, getting older you know. Everyone changes as they grow older." Cynthia's lips parted, her eyes still wide. "My God, Charlene, you actually sound like a man when you do that."

"I am a man, honey. Just call me Charley." Cynthia stared a moment longer, looked flustered, then jumped off the bed and grabbed Charlene's hand again. "Come on. We'll go down to the rumpus room in the basement and have drinks and chatter." Her movements were quick, but not so quick that Charlene missed the free, bouncing swing of the luscious breasts under the modest housecoat. She was thinking of that while Cynthia dragged her along. Maybe. Just maybe. Charlene remembered her bare feet as Cynthia tugged her toward the top of the stairs.

"Hey, I hope you haven't got splinters in these floors."
"

Oh no, Charlene. They're as smooth as silk." Then she wondered "Your feet aren't cold, are they?"

"No. The floor's warm enough. I just don't want to catch lockjaw or something."

"Don't worry about that. Come on." She tugged again at Charlene's hand. She started a headlong dash down the stairs but Charlene dragged her to a halt. "Hey, kid, you're forgetting your old man's advanced age. Take it easy. We'll get there - wherever *there* is."

"Sorry, Daddy." Cynthia smiled impishly up at Charlene's stem face. She slipped an arm around Charlene's waist, and Charlene felt the brush of a solid breast against her arm. "Let me help you, poor old Dad."

Charlene went along with it, slipping a suddenly palsied arm about the other girl. "Very well, child. Thank you very much." She gripped the tiny waist of the blonde, and enjoyed the touch immensely. This was indeed a dish.

From the ground floor they descended another flight of stairs to a narrow corridor with several doors opening off it.

"This used to be a huge old cellar until Daddy put rooms in it. We store all kinds of junk in most of them now." Cynthia stopped before one of the doors, swung it open and flicked a light switch. "This is what we call 'the relaxation room.' We can let our hair down here." She tittered. "At least I can." She shook her mop of shoulder-length nearly white blondeness, then ran her fingers through Charlene's short midnight hued hair. "You might have a little trouble with yours."

From the doorway, Charlene got a look at a cozy room, surprisingly large, but furnished for absolute comfort. There were several large lounge chairs, ottomans and a couple of low coffee tables. There was a small bar. There was a huge fireplace, dark now, and directly in front of the fireplace, almost in the center of the room, sat a low-backed divan at least eight feet long. And between the fireplace and the divan was stretched –

"Oh my God.. Not really." Charlene turned to Cynthia, pointing.

Cynthia giggled again. "Yep. Really. A polar bear rug. You see, my parents have some real square ideas about decorating." Then her tone changed. "You'd be surprised how comfortable it is to lounge around on. I used to flop there and chomp on popcorn and apples, · and read for hours."

"Oh, I wasn't criticizing. It's just that you read about them, and hear about them. But you never see them. At least I never did before."

"Well, now you have." Again the tugging hand. "Come on in. This rug's a lot softer than this hall floor." Charlene stepped in, and her feet sank into a soft, napped, wall-to-wall carpet of an eye-easing green color. She wiggled her toes luxuriously. "Hmmm, like crazy."
Cynthia waved a hand. "Sit down. What would you like to drink?"

"What is there?"

"Almost anything you want."

"Scotch and water for me. My tastes are simple." Then an idea struck her. "Why don't you park your seH on that sofa and let me do the honors. I love to mess around bars, and I don't get much chance to do It."

"Sure. Like you say, why not?" Cynthia bounced onto the divan and stretched her feet out, curling her toes in the bear skin. "I'll take the same as you." Charlene dug around the bar until she found the proper bottle and glasses, glanced over at Cynthia, saw she was still watching her toes in the bearskin rug, poured the glasses two-thirds full of Scotch, adding enough water to use as a defense against the chiding she knew was coming. She carried the drinks over, handed one to Cynthia, and sank down beside the girl. Cynthia looked at her glass, then at Charlene's. "No ice? There's some in the-"

''Who needs ice, with good whiskey?"

"Yeah. You're right. Well . . . " Cynthia raised her glass.

"Same to you."

They drank, and Cynthia sputtered, wiped her mouth, shook her head, and looked again at the glass. "Wow! I don't need ice, but I would like just a touch of water in this--this Molotov cocktail."

"That's exactly what you've got - a touch of water. Don't be a sissy, Sissy." Charlene took another nonchalant sip of her drink. Cynthia watched her lower the glass and smack her lips. "Well, if you can do it, so can I." She took a deep breath, tilted up the glass and took a quick gulp, concentrating on holding it down. She looked up at Charlene in triumph. "See?"

"Yeah, I see. Not much of a drinker, are you, Cynthia?"

Cynthia was embarrassed. "No, I guess not." "Well, don't let it buy you, baby. Lots of people   aren't."

"You drink as if you knew what it's all about, Charlene."

Charlene's faint smile showed. "Yeah, honey, I've had a little experience." Cynthia looked down at the glass in her hand again. "You know, I've got a nice warm feeling right here now." She rubbed her stomach. "It's not bad, once you get it down, even as strong as it is."

"Honey, if it's too strong, don't drink it."

"Oh, but I want to." She giggled lightly. "Can't have my guests showing me up." She took another quick gulp, with Charlene's black eyes watching closely. This time it seemed to go down easier, and Charlene smiled again.

"Well!" Cynthia took a deep breath, her face faintly flushed and her eyes sparkling. "Now we can talk." She smiled brightly at Charlene. But Charlene merely gazed blankly back at her, her face and body unmoving. "Charlene ... " No response. "W-what is it, Charlene? Why are you - " Charlene's voice cut in suddenly. "You're a very beautiful girl. Cynthia."

Cynthia blushed, and squirmed a little. "Well, thank you, Charlene. So-so are you." Her blush deepened and her eyes dropped, her hand picking imaginary lint off the divan. She looked up again. "What made you say that, Charlene?"
"Only the fact that you're beautiful, I thought you'd like to know."

"Oh." Cynthia took another gulp of her drink. "Well, uh, what'll we talk about first?" Charlene remained completely motionless. "Your breasts, Cynthia. Let's talk about your breasts."

"W-w-what? M-my breasts? Why in the world should -we - "

Again Charlene cut in "Because you're beautiful. Because *they're* beautiful. Why shouldn't we talk about them? Are they real, Cynthia?"

Cynthia gaped at her. "W-why of course they're real." Then she blushed again at the defensive tone that had • crept into her voice. Her blush became a• fiery red, and she took another gulp of her drink, nearly emptying the glass. She tried, not very successfully, to laugh. "Charlene, you - you're making fun of me, aren't you."

"Not at all, darling. I simply wondered if such lovely breasts could be real. I'm glad to know they are. Mine are, too, you know." And with the startled blue eyes on her, she casually drew aside the top of the robe, spread it wide. Her eyes watched closely, and her faint smile returned as she saw the little fist tighten around the glass, saw the lips move the slightest bit, and the pink tongue tip moisten the surface of those lips. She closed the robe as casually as she had opened it, raised her glass for another small sip.

She watched Cynthia gulp the last of her drink. After a short silence, Cynthia's eyes came back to Charlene's face, and Charlene noted a little tightening of the lips, an expectant look on Cynthia's face. Charlene would have bet that the girl was preparing to deny the request she expected to come, the request that she bare her own breasts to Charlene's gaze. But Charlene fooled her. She rose leisurely, took the empty glass out of Cynthia's hand and walked back to the bar, leaving her own nearly full glass· there, then returning to the divan with a comment about what a boring shift she had put in that night at the drive-in.

Cynthia was completely perplexed, and showed it. But Charlene chattered idly on, about nothing at all, making it entertaining, arid very· soon Cynthia was smiling again. Her smile was a little vacant now, and she tittered more and more frequently as Charlene went on with her mostly fictitious account of the day's and night's activities. Before she finished, she had Cynthia laughing freely and loudly, and not a little tipsily.

"Okay, Cynthia, now let's talk about you." "Me? What about me?" "Anything. Everything."

Cynthia glanced at the bar and giggled. "Let's have another drink. I feel wonderful now."
"Honey, take it easy. If we get really loaded we can't even talk sense. Enjoy the feeling you have, and forget the drinks for a while."

Cynthia giggled again. "Okay, Daddy. What do you want to know about me?" Charlene's eyes watched, then she smiled. "Well, why don't you tell me about your being scared?"

Cynthia's giggle quieted.

"Come on, Cynthia. Tell me about it." She moved her right hand across her bosom in two diagonal strokes. "Cross my heart, I'll never tell a soul." Then she leaned forward conspiratorially, whispered behind the back of her hand. "I'll tell you some real good ones about me, if you'll tell me your secrets." She giggled guiltily. "I got some dandies."

Cynthia laughed aloud at the burlesque. "Charlene, I can't keep up with you. Are you trying to keep me confused, or what?" Charlene spread her hands helplessly, looking as innocent as she could make it. "Wha'd I do, Mommy?" This brought another laugh. Charlene took advantage of it to repeat her request.

"Come on, Cynthia, let your hair down like you said we were going to do. Spill it."

Cynthia blushed again, hesitated, then laughed softly. "You know, it's funny now, when I think of it." She thought some more, laughed again, turned suddenly to Charlene. "Okay, I'll tell you, but you've got to promise you won't ever repeat it to anyone." Then her eyes were a little anxious. "And - and you won't laugh at me, will you, even if it does strike you funny?"

"Honey, if you don't want me to laugh, I won't laugh, I promise."

Cynthia studied her face for a moment, apparently accepted her sincerity, then giggled again. "Well, all right, here goes. It's not complicated. It's just that when I get scared I get -- sexy." Here her giggle was a little embarrassed.

"Sexy?"

The embarrassment deepened. "Yes. You know, passionate. Aroused."

"Really? You mean really shook?"

Another giggle. "And how. It makes me shiver just to think about it. Look . . . " She pushed back one sleeve of the housecoat and showed Charlene the goose flesh on her arm.

"Well, I'll be damned."

"Yeah, me too. And that's not the worst. Maybe it's because I'm so small or something, but when I get scared I can't run away. I find myself running toward whatever frightened me. Isn't that something? I go all to pieces. Once, when I was little, a big dog barked suddenly right behind me, and I turned and threw my arms around its neck. Of course I was too young to feel sexy then, but I kissed that dog, and I hugged him till my arms ached. And I pleaded with him not to hurt me. Lucky for me he was friendly. He was twice as big as I was. Then, when I got into my teens, I still couldn't resist the impulse, and the sexy thing got mixed up with it. I - I still can't resist."

"Like I said, maybe it's because I couldn't defend myself phys-ically, anyway, against something of any size at all, so I just throw myself on the mercy of whatever it is that scares me. And I suppose it's the old female coming out, when the sex bit enters the picture. Fear of death is supposed to make some people real sexy, from what I've heard. Well, any fear makes me that way."

She was tense during the recital, and her hands were twisting together in her lap, and Charlene was convinced that those knots were certainly back on the bosom under the housecoat. And the breasts were- probably feeling tight and heavy.

"Well, Cynthia, that's quite a situation."

"Yes, isn't it? What do you think about Charlene? What could I do to put a stop to it?"

"I don't know, honey. I'm no psych." She smiled slowly. "Maybe you just ought to take advantage of it. Enjoy it."

"*Enjoy* it?" Cynthia smiled faintly, through the pink of another blush. "That's the hell of it, I do, even when I'm shaking in my boots." Then, in a lower tone: "Or especially then." Charlene shook her head. "That's really quite a deal, Cynthia. Quite a deal." Then she straightened. "Well, we can't do anything about it tonight." Looking around the room, she spotted a small radio at the extreme end of the bar. "Hey, I didn't see that radio before. Does it work?"

"Yes, it works."

Charlene jumped up. "Well, let's have some music." She fiddled with the dial until she got some soft dance music, returned to the divan, bowed before Cynthia. "May I have this dance, miss?" Cynthia looked up, giggled, extended a languid hand. "Yes, of course." Then, as they moved silently over the thick carpet, she giggled again. "Maybe I ought to lead, being as big and powerful as I am."

Charlene looked down at her. "Okay, baby. We'll take turns." She leaned her cheek against the top of the girl's head, thinking of the tension that must have prompted the inane remark to which she had given an equally inane answer. She wondered whether now was the moment to put her already formed little plan for the rest of the evening into action. No, she decided. Wait a little while more.

They danced, mostly in silence, Charlene thoroughly enjoying the feel of the exquisite little body against her. They chattered about nothing at all, Charlene keeping the blonde in giggling expectation of the next witty remark. And finally Charlene decided to go into her act.

They were sitting again on the divan, the radio turned off now, and Charlene had just regaled her partner with a hilarious account of purely imaginary behind-the-barn episodes of her younger days. Then Charlene let her face settle into its frozen mask, eyes staring blankly ahead of her, while Cynthia's final laugh died away. There was a short pause, and another little titter from Cynthia. Another pause.

"Charlene.?"

Silence.

"Charlene . . . "

Still silence.

"What is it, Charlene?" She had to repeat the same question again before Charlene answered in a dead tone.

"Nothing, Cynthia, nothing."

"But why are you so quiet all of a sudden."

The black eyes turned their blank stare on Cynthia's face, kept it there in silence until the petite Cynthia began to squirm and look elsewhere, anywhere, except into those eyes.

"Please, Charlene. Y-you make me n-nervous."

Charlene stared a moment longer, then got up slowly and started walking the floor. She cast occasional blank stares at the girl on the divan, holding her eyes on Cynthia's face for long seconds at a time, sometimes turning her head over her shoulder while walking away, in order to keep her unblinking gaze on the white face. Cynthia giggled, twisted, tried to laugh. She tried every way she could think of to break that stony stare.

Nothing worked.

Now Charlene was walking toward the door of the room, and Cynthia wondered if she was leaving just like that.

"Charlene, are you going?"

No answer. At the door, Charlene turned, stared, walked back, stepping behind the divan. She returned to the door, again turned and stared. By now Cynthia was a nervous wreck, and her hands whipped up to cover her eyes, protect them from that burning, glassy stare. Her mouth opened in a little shriek. "Charlene! Stop it! *Please stop it!*" Her eyes were tightly closed, and her hands squeezed painfully against them. There was a dead silence, and when she finally took her hands away and opened her eyes the room was in absolute darkness·. Cynthia stared in horror, sobbed, whipped her hands up to rub her eyes, and stared again. Nothing but almost tangible darkness.

Oh God, she was blind! Her voice cracked in a shrieking *"CHARLENE!"* Silence. Unbearable, black silence. God, God, where was Charlene? Had she gone? What had happened to the lights? *"CHARLENE!"* Then she felt the warmth overwhelming her. She felt the blood pulsing in heavy waves through her, felt her body weakening with the urge to surrender to whatever was threatening it. She sobbed. Her words became despairing whispers. "Oh please, Charlene, please, please . . . "

Silence.

"Please, please please please please." Her whispers became

mere automatic murmurings.

Then the world seemed to explode around her as hands suddenly descended on her shoulders from behind. She uttered a piercing scream, which was cut off by the hands as they suddenly encircled her throat, tightening viciously. Helplessly, she felt her own hands come up to pat and stroke the backs of those clamped about her throat. As the hands loosened their clutch, she sobbed gratefully, turned her head to rub her cheeks against the rough cloth covering the arms that belong to those hands. Her lips strained to kiss the arms. Her whole body yearned toward the unknown assailant. Could it be Charlene? Or – or was it – Oh God!

Her head fell back limply, her eyes trying to see who might be standing over her. "Please ... please don't hurt me. Please please please ... "

The hands began to stroke lightly over her throat. Caressing, soothing. And the dead silence remained dead. "Charlene ... ?"

No response. Nothing but black silence and those hands crawling over her throat. Cynthia sobbed again, loudly. The hands tightened threateningly, and Cynthia's own hands moved faster against them, pleading mutely. Her lips parted to add verbal pleas to those of her hands, but the silence was broken by a sudden sharp whisper that tightened Cynthia's body painfully in shock. "Put your hands down!" Her hands fell like dropped stones to her sides, twitching, and her lips began to stutter frantically. "Y-y-yes. All r-right. A-anything. I'll do anything you say, anything you w-want. Only please don't hurt me. Please please please - " Her hysterical babbling was chopped short by another cutting whisper. "Shut up!" She sobbed gulping once more, and tried to remain perfectly still. The fear and the languorous warmth were weighing her down, and she felt her body sinking into complete helplessness.

It was that easy. Almost before Cynthia knew what was happening, Charlene had their garments stripped away and their bodies stretched luxuriously on the bearskin rug. And with the first artful touches of Charlene's skilled fingers on the engorged nipples of her breasts Cynthia became an eager accomplice in her own seduction. Cynthia's lips and fingers turned her into a wildly surging creature, avid to receive and give the exotic caresses that Charlene taught her. And Charlene taught her the value of restraint, of building tension until it exploded with incredible violence.

She taught her the weird thrill to be experienced only by complete surrender to the will of another. She taught her to wait for a sign or a word before making a move. She made Cynthia kneel between her feet and remain absolutely quiet while her toes explored the tiny body. She smiled to feel the vibration in the exquisite figure, the fight to restrain the urge that she knew was raging through the girl. And when she felt the restraint had reached its limit, she dropped her feet to the rug again. "All right, darling." Her smile widened and her face turned up to stare into the blackness overhead. She felt the tiny blonde fall forward with a sob of want, and the little hands clutched wildly.

It was a long night, a shattering night, and when it ended Cynthia Loomis was an abjectly eager vassal to the enigmatic Charlene Duval.

Or, as Charlene had also taught her, her darling Charley.

Ah yes, last night. But this was tonight, and the warm, rising wave within Charlene was not in her memory; it permeated her whole body, and she felt herself rising languorously on its crest, her body rocked gently, then harder. The wave was approaching the beach, where it would break suddenly and tumble her over and ·over, and leave her gasping for breath. Her hands smoothed Cynthia's soft shoulders, and her faint smile formed as she felt the signs of another rising wave in their tremble.

What a delicious little thing she was. How eager. How sweet. How... The wave suddenly tossed Charlene and her hands clutched convulsively at the white shoulders for support. But the little blonde needed support too. Her hands were clawing as desperately as Charlene's, and her muffled cry blended with Charlene's deep sighing groan.

They waited trembling, unmoving, until they were sure the violent wave had gone away, and then they opened their eyes and looked at each other.

Charlene stroked the blonde mop with a gentle hand. "You too, darling?"

"Yes, Charley." Cynthia's answer was a soft sigh. She scooted up to bury her face in Charlene's neck. "I love you, Charley. I love you."

"Yes, baby."

"D-do, you love me, too?"

Charlene stirred, pushed Cynthia away gently. "Get our clothes together, darling. It's late."

"B-but, darling - "

"Cynthia, please. Get our clothes."

Without another . word, Cynthia turned and started scrabbling for the carelessly dropped garments. She had a little trouble getting into hers, because the tears in he eyes made the poor visibility even worse. Charlene, however, had no such trouble. She had the car underway again, slowly and carefully this time, while Cynthia was still struggling to arrange herself properly.

SATAN WAS A LESBIAN

2

FUN WITH
TURKEY FEATHERS

I t was the eighth night since the first get-together with Cynthia, and Charlene was sleeping, deeply but uneasily. The eight nights had all been filled, until the early morning hours with Cynthia's warmth, her avid and complete surrenders, and Charlene had gone to bed tonight with a vaguely disturbed feeling about the situation. Why, she wondered, did their meetings seem to grow more and more delightful, instead of tapering off to an accustomed routine? She didn't like the idea. The dream in which she was now sunk was one she never remembered in her waking hours. It was also one that occurred fairly often, which made it all the more surprising that it should not be remembered. The elements in it were mainly a little black-haired, black eyed girl; a roughly dressed, rugged but kindly faced man, three tiny pure-white kittens; and a deep, nearly motionless creek.

The three kittens were in a brand new gunny sack carried in the man's hand as he walked toward the creek, completely unaware of the tot toddling along behind him. Once at the creek, he started to drop the bag into the water, hesitated, looked at the sack and muttered "Why ruin a good bag," and dumped the kittens out into the dark water. He shook his head, watched the mites struggle, heard their faint, thin, strangled mewing, watched their bodies finally float motionless. He retrieved the tiny bodies, still shaking his head, and laid them out on the bank.

Straightening, he snapped his fingers lightly, remembering what he had forgotten to bring. He turned back up the path, nearly tripping over   the silent little figure standing there with her wide eyes fixed on the unmoving kittens. "Oh my God, honey. What are you doing here?"

He knelt beside her, trying to distract her gaze from the three water—soaked corpses. She moved aside, but kept the black eyes fixed on their targets, speaking in a piping little voice. "What 'cha doin'?"

He tried to explain that her daddy had ordered him to drown the three "little nuisances." Then he tried to answer her question as to what "drowning" was. Then of course he had to try to explain what "death" was, and how it came to everything and everybody eventually. He even had to try to explain what "kittens" were. He found himself at a complete loss, however, when he had to go into reasons why her daddy considered them "nuisances."

"An' they was 'kittens?'"

"Yes, honey, they were kittens. Babies, honey. Like you, only different. Baby animals. Not nearly as important as baby people."

"An' someday you an' me'll be like that?"

"Yes, honey. Someday everybody will be like that. We'll all be gone."

"Gone? Are they gone now?"
"Well — well yes, baby. They've gone away. They're not here any more."
"Then what's that?" The tiny finger pointed. "Well, honey, that's . . . that's just their bodies. That's . . . well, you might say that's nothing at all."

She was looking up into his face now, very solemnly.
"An' if I held 'em now, I'd be holdin' nothin'?"
"Yes, baby. But you — you can't hold 'em now. You can't hold "nothin'"; I have to bury them." He took her hand and led her

away up the path. "I have to get a shovel and bury them."

"Bury 'em?"

"Yes. You see, now that they're nothing, I have to put them in the ground." Then he cursed under his breath and dropped to his knees. "Tell me, honey, did you like 'em? Did you know about 'em before — before I..."

She nodded once, glanced again at the bedraggled little bodies at the edge of the creek. "*I liked 'em. They was soft an' pretty. An' they liked me, too. They'd hug me when I picked 'em up. They was nice and warm and fuzzy.*"

The man cursed again to himself. He cursed the playboy employer who'd ordered the drowning, he cursed himself for not suspecting a possible connection between the habitually silent and unsmiling little girl and the three kittens. He studied the small face before him, trying to find some clue to the child's reaction. He tried to smile. "You'll soon forget 'em, honey. After all, they were only three days old. You couldn't like 'em too much, could you?" His eyes looked a little strained.

She ignored the question — She looked again at the three little bodies. "An' now they're nothin'."

"Well yes, honey, they're — "

But she had turned and started up the path again, away from the creek bank with its "nothin'," leaving him to trail along behind, wondering what to say or do, wondering whether the child was indifferent, or heart broken, wondering whether he or anyone else would ever understand the almost sphinx—like mystery of little Charlene.

Now, years later, in the darkness of Charlene's bed room, the scene came to life again. Charlene's body twisted restlessly and an incoherent mumbling came from her sleeping throat, followed by words spoken with startling clarity in the voice of a very small girl: "An' now they're nothin'."

No sooner had the last word sounded than Charlene's eyes snapped open and her body froze to a dead quiet. She tensed, as if listening to a very faint sound. She frowned, shook her head, wondering what had awakened her with such a jolt. She lay absolutely motionless, her eyes fixed on the darkness above her, the slight frown on her brow. Then her eyes turned to the open window, watching the faint glow of the stars in the clear sky. The frown deepened. What had awakened her? Thoughts of Cynthia again?

What was she going to do about the girl and her endless avowals of love? Mentions of love were things that Charlene tried to avoid whenever possible. They disturbed her. The very thought disturbed her. And Cynthia —

She shook her head in irritation. Later. Now was not the time to think about anything like that. She turned on her side, closed her eyes, willing herself to return to sleep. Then she turned on her other side. Then onto her back. She cursed softly. Sleep, damn it, go to sleep. She sat up, hugging her knees, scanning the dark outlines of distant trees through the open window, looking up again toward the stars. Damn it, she had to do something. Cynthia.

She cursed again, forced her thoughts to the activities of the day. And her lip curled. What in hell was there in the day's activities to keep her mind off — yes, damn it — Cynthia. She tried to think about the future. No good either. Too nebulous. Who knows the future, especially if he — or she — is not particularly interested in it? The present, then. But all she could think of concerning the present was the fact that she wanted to go back to sleep. She lay back down and closed her eyes, forcing her body to relax. Nothing doing.

Then a thin smile formed on her lips. The past, then. The past held plenty of interesting things to keep her mind off —

Another curse. She absolutely refused to think any more about — Then the smile was back. Mary Anne! That's it. Think about Mary Anne! No complications there — but plenty of delightful memories! And it was all behind her, so there was no vexing worry about solutions.

Mary Anne …

Charlene had finished high school well behind others of her own age. She had attended school in a small town where the ruling powers had little time for the idea of shoving a student through regardless of accomplishment. If the student didn't master the subject in one semester, he repeated it, no ifs, ands, or buts. Charlene had had to repeat several, both in grammar school and high school.

And when she finally finished, she was better educated than most of her teachers. Not in the subjects they taught, naturally enough, but in subjects dealing more directly with life and its problems, its questions and answers. She could not be called erudite, perhaps, but she had a cold, practical knowledge and outlook that most pie never acquire.

She had developed a fascination with death in her early years. Almost as soon as she could read she began to spend almost all of her spare time in the town library. She knew Omar Khayyam's *Rubaiyat* word for word, and she probably remembered *Thanatopsis* better than Bryant himself ever had. She read various theories of the hereafter, of reincarnation, of every available thinker on the subject of death and its follow ups. From that she branched out into the life sciences: biology, physiology, psychology, botany, and all the others she could find. A lot of it she didn't understand, but a lot of it she did. When she was not in the library or in school, or attending to her duties at home, she was in the fields, woods, swimming or wading in the creek, studying the life forms in and under the water. She had her own microscope in her own room of the house, and she spent hours over it. The creek, however, of all her sources of material, held a special fascination for her.

Why, she couldn't have said. But it did. The fascination was not a pleasant one, but it was powerful, and she was utterly unable to avoid it. And with characteristic intensity she tried to understand it. However, this was one of the few things that completely. baffled her. Another was the fact that sometimes she felt an almost painful aversion to old Curt Jenkins, the man who, together with his wife, had been responsible for her care since the death of her parents in a plane crash when she was about six years old.

She hadn't been particularly upset about her parents' going. After all, she'd hardly known them. They were constantly on the go, leaving the care of her and the farm to old Curt and his wife Martha. Both of them loved her deeply and tried every way they knew to understand her and give her the love she lacked from her parents. She appreciated their efforts, and loved them both as deeply as she could love anybody; but as she grew older she realized that they probably never knew it. At her parents' death, Curt and "Aunt" Martha became her guardians; the farm was hers, administered by the couple.

She grew to her final five-feet-eight, a lithe, panther-like figure with soft outlines, full, round breasts as firm as air cushions. All in all, hers was a body to more than satisfy the more critical of panting male requirements, and one to arouse the most virulent of envies among women.

Strangely enough, however, no panting male ever had the pleasure of that body. Most of them showed a mixture of fascination and fear around her. It was not physical fear, rather, like a fear shown by children for spooks and hobgoblins. Though none of them would admit it, they felt the urge to run and hide from her whenever she got close. And, studying the lushness of her body they scratched their heads and wondered what in hell was wrong with them — or her.

Girls, on the other hand, seemed to feel the same fascination mixed with more awe than fear. They looked at her with shining eyes. They felt like squirming when she was near; some of them actually did squirm, trying hard to cover up by pretending to stretch, to change position from sitting to standing. In private, they too scratched their heads, wondering what was wrong with them — or her.

Charlene knew vaguely a little about what bothered the girls. She knew the silently screaming urges that possessed women at bullfights, though she had never seen one and the same urges showed themselves at prize fights or wrestling matches, making themselves evident in the glittering of the eyes, the panting breath, the twisting of the body, and the actual, physical screaming of the women at the height of violent and bloody action. She knew, from her reading in psychology and from her own shrewd intuition, the sexual basis of such urges and behavior. She knew something, strictly on the academic level, about lesbians and their methods and practices. But she was too busy to think too much or worry about unimportant things like that.

She didn't understand the boys' reactions at all. Why a boy should fear her was beyond her comprehension. Well, there was one ... She had caught a sixth-grade classmate pulling the pigtails of a wailing little girl one day, and he had planted her fist squarely on his nose, with all her considerable power behind it. He might well have reason to fear her. But the others? Well, she didn't have time to worry about that either. There was too much studying to be done. So much, paradoxically, that it interfered with her school work as well as her social life.

So, by the time Charlene finished high school she had a mind of her own, kept her own counsel (as she always had), thought like an adult of *well* beyond her years. All she lacked was practical experience in living among strangers. This became her next project. She broached the subject one warm summer night at the supper table, to be met with shocked looks from Curt and his wife.

"What? A girl your age running out just like that? What would you do? Where would you go? It's unthinkable!"

Charlene looked calmly from one to the other. "Have I ever given you any reason to think that I'm irresponsible? That I can't take care of myself?"

Curt snorted. "Honey, you don't have any idea of. what you'd meet up with away from home."

"I don't exactly agree with you. But suppose I did. How will I ever find out, if I stick here with you? I'll have to find out eventually by going out to meet whatever might come along. Why not now?"

"Because, honey, you're too young. Look at what you've got here. You own this farm. There's every thing here, or near here, that anyone could ever want. Why should you run off somewhere? What would happen to the farm?"

"I should think you'd know by now, Curt, that as far as I'm concerned it's your farm. And it will remain your farm as long as you want it. What would I do with it? I don't even like farming. And if I did, I'm a woman. How would I run it?

"As for my being young — well, there's nothing I can do about that. But I'm as big and strong as I'll ever be right now. I believe my thinking is as good as it will be until I have some experience behind me to temper it. Besides, I wasn't thinking of going to China or India or some other place like that. I just want to live alone, make my own decisions, depend on nobody but myself. Please, Curt, think about it. I might only go ten miles away. But I'd be strictly on my own."

"Of course I'd let you know where I was, so you'd have no cause for worry. And if anything drastic happened, something beyond my ability to handle, I could always come home. And, to repeat, I'm sure I've never given you any cause to doubt my ability to take care of myself, or to question my sense of responsibility."

Curt squirmed in his chair, looked at his wife. "I still don't like it. Mama, what do you think?"

"I just don't know either." She looked at Charlene, brightened. "Honey, why don't you decide where you want to go? Then we can talk it over and settle it. Besides, that'd give Curt and me a chance to sort of get used to the idea of your not being here. It'd be kind of strange, you know, with just us two here. We'd miss you like the very devil."

Charlene smiled at the two of them. "Good enough." Three days later, she was unpacking her bags in a rented room of an old house in a small town some twenty-five miles from the farm. Two days after that she had a job as night ticket taker and usherette at the local movie house, hired by a nervous manager who couldn't seem to take his eyes off her during the interview, and who showed the familiar symptoms of not wanting to get too close to her. Charlene hid a smile at the thought that wolves were not likely to be among her major problems.

Her thought about wolves had covered only the male of the species, however. She had forgotten that there are females of all species, including wolves. It's quite likely that Mary Anne Adams had never thought of herself as a wolf before, but she became very much aware of the tendency the first time she laid eyes on Charlene Duval. She saw in Charlene the very essence of wolf-ish appeal, and she felt her own wild urge to mate with it.

She walked to the door, unable to keep from staring at the tall, quiet figure whose hand was extended personally for her ticket. She looked down at that hand, fantasizing wild scenes, then glanced up to see the black eyes fixed on her face. The fantasy grew. And when Charlene took the ticket from her, brushing her hand inadvertently, she felt her knees flex.

Charlene looked thoughtfully at the girl as she threaded her way to a seat. Then she returned to the front door, not smiling as she usually did upon encountering the unmistakable symptoms shown by so many women and girls. The glistening eyes, the damp lips, the wide eyes — everything was the same. But there was something else. Charlene had felt a deep tugging within herself. She tried to analyze it. The girl was a few inches shorter than herself, full bodied, with features usually described as pretty and sensual. Her breasts and legs were perfect. Her hair was dark brown, as were her eyes, soft—looking and rich in texture. Her skin glowed with youth and health, and she moved with con-trolled energy. She was a beautifully striking picture. But all this Charlene had seen before. That couldn't explain the internal tug.

She frowned, concentrating. But then business began to pick up for the second showing of the film, and Charlene forgot the inci-dent in the rush of work. As the last showing got well under way, Charlene was free to go. She stopped in a small drugstore coffee shop for an egg sandwich and a cup of coffee. Then she frowned over the food, thinking again about her reaction to the girl.

Charlene went to sleep that night, the glowing face was the last thing to leave her consciousness. She still hadn't analyzed her own unexpected inward roil. The next night the girl was back, apparently feeling some need to explain that she couldn't help seeing the picture again, her face flushed and her eyes trying not to stare too obviously. Charlene smiled her faint smile and agreed that the film was well worth seeing again. The third night, Charlene saw her walk past the theater several times, now on this side of the street, now on the other, her eyes always on the front door. Once, Charlene returned to her post after showing a customer to a seat; she saw the girl standing motionless in front of the theater, her body looking tense. The girl, however, seeing Charlene watching her, suddenly turned and walked away. Charlene smiled again.

On the fourth night the program changed, and Mary Anne Adams was the first in line at the box—office. She didn't come out when the first show ended. Then, as Charlene was getting ready to leave during the second showing, Mary Anne just "happened" to be leaving at the same time. She showed a proper amount of surprise and pleasure, introduced herself, and suggested that the two of them stop in for a "malt or something."

Charlene smiled, nodded. In the drug store booth, they got better acquainted with each other, Mary Anne doing most of the talking, face pink, eyes shining, trying hard to hide her nervousness. Charlene listened, smiled, nodded. Then Mary Anne made a sudden move as if to put her hand on Charlene's, flushed and drew back again, leaned forward and spoke in an excited tone.

"I've just had a great idea. Our place has a small lake on it, completely private. Why don't we go out there tomorrow and go swimming? We can laze around in the sun. We can take a picnic lunch along and have ourselves a ball all day. How about it?" Charlene considered for a moment, accepted with smiling thanks, and agreed that it would be a wonderful chance for relaxation and fun.

Mary Anne's "place" was a farm just at the edge of town, considerably larger than Charlene's, and at ten o'clock the next morning Charlene was walking briskly up toward the house, swinging a towel and bathing suit. She'd walked from her rented room, and felt great. Mary Anne answered her knock almost as if she had been standing just inside the door waiting for it. She introduced Charlene to her mother, a busy woman with a harassed look about her face. Charlene wondered briefly whether the look was the result of overwork, or worry about her daughter. Her daughter was one girl who might well be worried about.

Mary Anne was wrapped in a thick green terrycloth robe that seemed to be big enough to go around her twice, engulfing her like a lush growth of shrubbery from throat to sneaker-clad feet. She grabbed Charlene's hand and pulled her like a tug towing a barge. "Come on, you can change in my room. I've got another robe like this one, and you can wear it down to the beach. No sense walking a quarter of a mile in all those clothes."

Inside her room, Mary Anne showed signs of wanting to wait around while Charlene changed, but finally backed to the door. "I'll go and finish packing the lunch while you get into your suit. "The robe's in the closet right there." She pointed. "Hurry up ·will you? The sun's going to waste." She left, reluctantly, closing • the door behind her.

A few minutes later the two green-wrapped figures were trudging down a narrow lane away from the house and toward a grove of trees some distance to the west. Mary Anne was explaining that the lake was set in the middle of the grove, that there was a lovely narrow beach of fine sand, backed by tall fragrant grass covering a sizable flat-surfaced clearing.

"Sounds like an ideal spot for a nudist camp."

"It is." Mary Anne laughed mischievously. "For one — or sometimes two. I have a girlfriend who comes over once in a while, and we come out here — " She hesitated, blushing. "Well, Mama doesn't like me to run around nude in front of people, but what's the difference ... I .mean ... when we're both girls and ... and good friends? Mama doesn't even like me to wear the kind of bathing suits I always buy. Mama's kinda old fashioned, I guess." By now Mary Anne was so flustered that she didn't even seem to know what she was saying, and Charlene laughed softly.

"Don't flip, Mary Anne. Mama's not here now, and I don't care if you walk down Main Street in your birthday suit. Might even stir up a little excitement for a change."

Mary Anne giggled. "It's a thought."

They walked in silence for a minute or so. Then Charlene stopped, tugging on the handle of the picnic basket swinging between them. "Wait a minute." They set the basket down, and Charlene untied the belt of her robe. "This thing gets heavy." She shrugged out of the garment, slung it over her shoulder and picked up one handle of the basket. "Okay, let's go." But Mary Anne simply stared at Charlene's sleek body, encased in its well—fitted but unfrilly two-piece nylon swimsuit. "My God, Charlene, you look as smooth as a seal in that outfit. I'll bet you swim like one too, don't you? You — you're absolutely magnificent." Then she blushed again and bent quickly to grab the other handle of the basket.

Charlene chuckled. "Thank you, dear. I'm wondering what you look like. What kind of suit are you wearing?" Mary Anne giggled again. "You'll see, when we get to the beach. Or at least out of sight of the house. I wouldn't want Mama to see me and start shaking her head again."

Then minutes passed, then as they came out on the shore of a beautiful sylvan lake glittering bluely in the bright sunshine, it was Charlene's turn to stare. They set the basket down on the sand and Mary Anne shrugged out of her robe, spreading it out in the tall grass she'd described earlier.

"See, green robe, no grass stains." She straightened to see Charlene gazing at her. And she squirmed. Those black eyes seemed to be absorbing her into their depth. She glanced down at the skimpy tan-colored bikini that would have caused blushes on the Riviera. She looked up again, trying to read the expression on Charlene's face, but found it impossible. She squirmed again, giggled tensely. "See why Mama frowns on my suits?"

"Yes, I do." Charlene's voice was low. Mary Anne turned away suddenly, bent and fumbled unnecessarily   with the green robe, straightening out imaginary folds and wrinkles. She stood upright again, her face pink, and said, "Well, come on, let's try the water." She turned and ran, splashing out to knee depth and diving smoothly, surfacing some distance out and blowing like a whale.

"Come on, Charlene." Charlene waved a hand. "Coming, Mother." She ran in tum, her mind's eye still seeing those plump active breasts and lush hips, those long, full thighs and round buttocks moving sensuously as Mary Anne went through her fumbling with the robe. She thought she knew now what had caused that internal turmoil the first night she'd seen Mary Anne. It was surely an animal response to the girl.

Well, well, well...

They played, splashed, dived, hunting along the bottom of the warm water for buried treasures such as crayfish, minnows, colorful pebbles. And they eyed each other covertly. They played tag, and Mary Anne's touches seemed to linger. Charlene began to show her faint smile, and made her touches deliberately short and light, and she felt Mary Anne quiver under every one. She saw the girl's cheeks take on a pink tinge that failed to fade, saw the shine in the brown eyes grow brighter and brighter. • She felt the tension increase between the two of them. They played, they watched, and the warmth of the sun seemed to grow and grow and grow. At least, they pretended that it was the sun's warmth.

Then Mary Anne splashed water in Charlene's face. Charlene blinked, wiped the water from her eyes. "Look here, kid, you pull that again and I'll whop your fanny for you."

Mary Anne hesitated, eyes widening as she looked at Charlene. Then, in a voice that sounded a little squeaky, she said, "You and who else?" Another hesitation, and she splashed again, then turned with a squeal and headed for shore as Charlene lunged for her. Charlene followed. Mary Anne looked over her shoulder, squealed again, and started running toward the tall grass beyond the beach. She looked back again. Then she stumbled and fell to her hands and knees, letting out a shriek.

Charlene noted that the girl had stumbled at just the right point to fall onto the spread-out robe. "Hmm, how coincidental." She pounced, pinning Mary Anne face down on the robe. Mary Anne squealed again, putting up a struggle that seemed strangely ineffective for a girl of her robust health and physique. Charlene quickly slid her feet under the girl's body and drew the threshing figure up so that the plump buttocks were handy to her good right hand, holding Mary Anne down with her left hand planted between the girl's shoulders. She drew back her right arm, ready for the first spat. She stopped the swing and noted that the infinitesimal bra of the bikini was hanging limply around the svelte waist, loosened by the wild bounce of the girl's breasts in her running or in the "struggle" on the robe. She saw the lovely legs still kicking, but with no real authority. She felt the girl's body tense in anticipation of the first blow.

And she waited.

Mary Anne turned her face toward Charlene, wondering. Then Charlene's right hand came down in four quick, sharp little spats on the bare under-curve of the plump buttocks, just above the juncture with the thighs. Mary Anne squealed again, huskily this time.

Charlene paused, feeling the increased tremble in the prone body, the heaving of heavy breathing under the hand on the girl's back. She raised her right hand again, glanced at the side of the face buried in the robe. Reaching out deliberately she undid the knots that held the slim excuse for trunks together. She stripped away the trunks, leaving the soft expanse on her lap as bare as the sand on the beach. During this operation, Mary Anne's breathing seemed to stop completely, but she showed no other sign of awareness of what was happening.

When it started again, her breathing. was even more ragged than before; Charlene's hand came down again, this time with plenty of force and sting.
One, two . . . six . . . eight . . . ten. Mary Anne's fanny turned a bright pink. Then Charlene leaned back indolently on her elbows, watching. Mary Anne lay trembling for a moment, then her head

turned to look questioningly at Charlene's little smile. She stirred, rubbed her buttocks, still looking at Charlene, her tongue coming out to moisten her lips. She sat up, on Charlene's lap, seemingly unaware of her nudity except for the thin band around her waist. She gave a little lunge, one arm going around Charlene's neck, the other around her back. She buried her face in Charlene's shoulder, mumbling softly against it, "You're *mean*."

Charlene smiled wider, sat up and glanced down to see one bare breast nestled warmly in her cleavage, quivering as if with a life of its own. She slipped her arms around Mary Anne, stroking her back. "Yep. That's what everybody tells me." Her hands stroked higher, then lower, from the shoulders to the round hips. Then paused to untie the knot in the band at Mary Anne's waist, casting it aside. They stroked some more, over the hips to the thighs, circling from back to front, front to back, slipping lightly over the warmth back up. to the shoulders. She felt Mary Anne's lips moving moistly against her shoulder, then the teeth gripping lightly.

Mary Anne finally raised her head and looked into Charlene's eyes from inches away. She brought her face to Charlene's, and for the first time in her life Charlene felt the moist, melting kiss of a thoroughly aroused woman applied to her lips. The questing tongue came into play, and Charlene's long-developed self control was taxed to its fullest powers to keep her hands stroking evenly over the girl's lushness.

Mary Anne drew back again. "You — you haven't done much kissing in your life, have you, Charlene." "No. Mary Anne, I haven't." A calm statement of fact

"I'll teach you."Mary Anne's reply was anything but calm as she proceeded to give the lesson of her life.

For the next few minutes there was only soft whispering of instructions and long periods of eager demonstration. When Mary Anne's head went back to rest on Charlene's shoulder, her body was in an almost constant state of tremor. Charlene was an amazing pupil and a quick learner.

Charlene glanced down at the velvety breast snuggled so cozily between the upper slopes of her own. She could feel the nipple poking into her flesh, and the sensation was delightful. Her eyes moved up to the side of the throat, arched as Mary Anne's cheek lay on her shoulder, the flushed face cuddled against the side of her neck.· She watched the thumping, erratic pulse in the girl's neck, and saw a drop of water standing directly on the thudding surface. She bent her head, her lips parting according to Mary Anne's instructions. The parted lips settled warmly and tightly, and then the tongue flashed like that of a chameleon after an insect, snapping up the drop of water and bringing a sudden lunge to Mary Anne's whole body. A drop of water on one shoulder. Again the lips settled and again the tongue flashed. Another lunge from Mary Anne. This time she sat up and looked wildly at Charlene. "God, Charlene — " Charlene's hand closed softly over her lips. "Shhh." Charlene's eyes were fixed on Mary Anne's heaving left breast. There was a water drop working its way toward the erect tip, and Charlene's eyes followed its course closely. When it finally arrived at its destination Charlene went after it.

This time Mary Anne's body convulsed and she gave a little scream of pure ecstasy. Charlene gripped her tighter, her eyes moving to the right breast in search of another bit of moisture. Her eyes scanned Mary Anne, then she pushed the girl clear of her body and stood up, taking Mary Anne by the hand. "Come on, darling, we've been out of the water too long."

"B—b—but — "

"Come on now. Don't argue." She led" Mary Anne down to the lake, walking steadily out into the water until it was up to Mary Anne's neck. Then she turned around and came back to shore, still towing the girl by the hand. Mary Anne's eyes were literally bugging out now, and her face was filled with such wonder that Charlene chuckled as she stopped by the green robe and urged her partner down onto it. "Don't worry, Mary Anne. I'm not crazy." She looked at the body stretched out on the robe, the eyes wide and questioning. "At least not completely — not yet." She sank to her knees beside the supine Mary Anne, leaned over her with a hand on either side of the girl's body. "I've just discovered a lovely new game of treasure hunting." Her eyes swept the body once more, with its glittering myriad water particles. "Your part of the game is to lie perfectly still and let me hunt."

The hunt began. The lips pressed and the tongue flicked, and Mary Anne twitched with each thrust. On and on it went, with a pause now and then while Charlene pushed Mary Anne's clutching hands down to her sides on the robe. "No, no. You're to lie perfectly quiet. If you can't follow the rules, we'll have to stop playing."

Charlene started hunting again. Mary Anne tried valiantly to lie still but the game was interrupted from time to time despite her efforts. She was a quaking wreck when Charlene finally drew back from the rigidly pointing nipples and looked down at her, her smile completely gone now. The black eyes swept downward, over Mary Anne's flat, toned midsection. Charlene whispered in a husky voice "Your tummy's a veritable oasis for a thirsty hunter, what other nectars do you have for me." Her head dipped again and plunged into Mary Anne.

Mary Anne closed her eyes tightly, gripped the robe with such force that her fingers ached, trying frantically to prevent her body from arching and twisting. She bit her lips so hard that a trickle of blood started. Her breasts were exploding with so much excitement that they started to ache and she finally was forced to cup her hands over them to try to ease the pain.

Charlene's lips had slowed, then they stopped their wandering completely and settled down for an extended stay between Mary Anne's legs having found an abundant supply of what she was after. Her legs opened wider as Charlene pressed tighter between them. Her tongue flicked faster and harder. Mary Anne had completely forgotten the rules of the game as she twisted, lunged, arched, clawed, squealed, screamed, moaned, squealed again and again and again and again.

Her body became an upward arched bow, supported only. at head and heel, helped by the tight grip of Charlene's hands on the tensed, quivering buttocks.

"Charlene! Stop, please! Oh God, darling, please, *please stop!*"

But Charlene didn't stop. Her grip tightened and held fast, until the savagely moving body beneath her lips slumped into inertness, the gasping mouth uttering a helpless, hopeless sound of complete collapse. There was a long, silent moment of unmoving stillness. Then Charlene raised her head and released her grip. She slid up to take Mary Anne's hands in her own and lower them to the girl's sides again. She cupped her own hands on the heaving breasts, moving them in slow circular motion around them. She pressed a lingering kiss in the warm valley between the white mounds, whispering "I'm sorry, darling . . . " she said as she kissed Mary Anne's smooth throat "I didn't want to miss a single drop . . . " Her lips closed softly on the lobe of Mary Anne's ear. "Not... one... delicious... drop." Then she lay back on the robe, slipped one arm under Mary Anne's neck, cradling the girl's head on her shoulder.

Again there was silence, broken only by faint splashing from the lake and occasional distant bird. Charlene's eyes moved to look at the surroundings, and it occurred to her that anyone seeing their activities would have gotten a pretty good show, however the grass was so high that a person would have to stand directly over them to see them at all. Her faint smile came again as she entertained herself with the expression on the face of a possible onlooker.

She closed her eyes again, still smiling, and relaxed into an almost trance-like state of quiet and peace. Her nerves had been jumpy from her novel experience, and she enjoyed the deliberate effort she had to exert to quiet them, absolute command of herself was one of the things she'd always prized highly among her skills, and now she concentrated on maintaining it. The warm body pressed lightly against her side was no help, but the harder a task, the more Charlene enjoyed it. She smiled wider and relaxed more.

Mary Anne lay quietly beside her until the young and vigorous body recouped its strength, a matter of no great difficulty in view of the stimulating presence of Charlene so close beside her. She finally moved one thigh, sliding it gently against Charlene's, slipped it up and over her. Then she half-sat up, leaning over

Charlene, watching the closed eyes. Charlene showed no sign of awareness, even when Mary Anne whispered, "Darling, you're a complete devil, aren't you."

Mary Anne's hand trailed lightly over Charlene's neck, down toward the rise of her breast. Then she frowned, as she glanced down. "Charlene, you've still got your suit on. That's not fair." She giggled. "I hadn't even noticed it before."

Charlene opened her eyes then. "You were too busy, darling." Another giggle. "Yes, I guess I was." Her hands began to fiddle with the top of the suit. "Let me take it off for you." Charlene grabbed her hands, stopping them. "No." She felt a disagreeable sensation at the thought of letting Mary Anne take control, even for a moment. Mary Anne's whisper was disappointed.

"But why not, darling? I want to see your breasts, all of you." Her voice took on a mock shocked tone. "I'll bet you're flat-chested! All that bulge is courtesy of the U.S. Rubber Company."

Charlene laughed. "Good pitch, Mary Anne, but it won't get the job done." She still held Mary Anne's hands, and now she raised them and looked at them. She looked up at Mary Anne's soft, full lips. She wondered what those hands and lips could and would do to her and she decided that deliberate surrender to them would still leave her in actual control of the situation.

She shrugged, let go of the hands. "Well, maybe after all . . . " She closed her eyes again, felt Mary Anne's hands busy themselves, lifting and turning her. She felt the cool rush of air over her suddenly naked breasts, then the feather-light touches of fingers and palms closed warmly over them, squeezed.

Mary Anne's lips came down on the upright nipples, and a tongue tip touched them lightly, then harder, circling. Charlene felt her body start a slow undulation, and she made an effort to stop it. Then, with the lips still at her breasts, she felt the hands slipping down over her stomach to work on the trunks of her suit. She turned lazily to help the hands in their work, still fighting to keep her body from moving except as she willed it. She felt another rush of cool air, felt the trunks being slipped off over her feet. Then she felt the warmth of Mary Anne's naked body slithering along the length of her own until the girl was resting completely upon her. She felt Mary Anne's lips close on hers, felt the tongue slip between her lips and begin a slow, thorough search. Under the soft pressure of the curved body and the sensuous action of the educated mouth, the battle for immobility was almost impossible. She finally forced her mouth to stop responding to the kiss, and Mary Anne's soft lips moved away, down over her neck to her breasts, her stomach, the tongue still searching. Charlene felt herself weakening. She reached down and cupped Mary Anne's face in her hands, lifting it forcibly from her body. "Darling, I haven't got a drop of water on me."

Mary Anne frowned puzzledly, then grinned suddenly. "Water? Who needs it? All I need is you and you won't be dry for long." She seemed to sense Charlene's need for control now, and she waited patiently until the hands on her face loosened the hold, dropping back to the robe. Then her lips went back to work, her hands reaching up to squeeze Charlene's breasts with a steady caressing movement.

Charlene felt control slipping further and further from her. Her hands came up to rest on the backs of Mary Anne's, slid slowly up along the length of the round arms to the shoulders, back down to the hands. It was wonderful, what Mary Anne was doing, and Charlene slowly lost all concern about control or lack of it. Her body was ignoring her commands completely, going on its own twisting, surging way, obeying only the orders of Mary Anne's imperative lips and squeezing hands. Charlene experienced another first. Behind her tightly closed lids she seemed to see the rising of a great green sea waves around her feet. It washed higher over her, warm and comforting and at the same time excruciatingly exciting, and it rose higher and higher despite her weak efforts to keep it back. Now it was closing over her head and she was gasping, sputtering, squirming frantically, her hands clutching wildly at whatever she could find as a possible support and help in her struggles. She seemed to feel seaweed under her wildly flailing fingers and she clutched it viciously. Then, as her breath seemed to be completely spent, the wave tossed her and slowly sank back into the sea from which it had come. Charlene waited tensely for it to return, but finally opened her eyes. Then she saw that the seaweed in which her fingers were still tangled was Mary Anne's hair, and she heard the girl voicing pained protests.

Charlene loosened her grip and her eyes roved. No sea. Nothing but green grass and robe, and bright sun overhead. She breathed a deep sigh and closed her eyes again. Mary Anne moved up beside her again, with the other robe in her hands. She spread it over the two of them with a whisper, "We don't want too much sun, do we?" Then she cuddled close to Charlene, one arm draped over Charlene's body, and they drifted off into dreamland.

Charlene awoke first, with a feeling of suffocation. She threw off the robe that had covered them from head to foot, and looked down at herself, then at Mary Anne. They were both streaming with perspiration, and their bodies were plastered together by it. Her movements awoke Mary Anne, who looked up at her sleepily, then let her gaze follow Charlene's. Her eyes came more awake, and she threw her arms around Charlene, hugging her tightly. "Time for another treasure hunt, darling?"

Charlene pulled her arms away, spatted her smartly on the rump, and jumped to her feet. "Time to get into that lake and cool off." She took off at a run, followed by Mary Anne's amused laugh, then by the girl herself. Mary Anne came up behind her as she was treading water, slipped her hands around and over Charlene's breasts. "Party-pooper."

Charlene pulled her hands away again. "You are a depraved, insatiable female. Come on, let's get to that lunch. I'm starved." Mary Anne snickered. "Already?" Then she headed for shore, leaving Charlene for once trying to think of a suitable reply.

The lunch was delicious, and the iced tea slid down their parched throats like nectar. And they talked. At least Mary Anne did, Charlene said no more than she felt necessary. Mary Anne was too free with her conversation for Charlene's taste. In answer to Charlene's questions, the girl freely admitted previous activities such as they had just enjoyed. She just as freely told the name of, and described, the girl who had taught her all of her considerable skills in such matters. They picked up the leavings of the lunch, lazed on the robes in the sun, took another relaxing dip, and finally set out on the way back to Mary Anne's, Charlene having found out the answers to all the questions she could think of at the time.

At the house, Mary Anne tried to persuade Charlene to stick around for a while. Failing that, she tried to pin Charlene down on a future date for another "party" but Charlene thought of Mary Anne talking about other girls, and purposely left things very vague as to what might happen later. On the way back to her room, she wondered how long it would be before her name was known, along with her newly acquired skills, to others in the town.

It didn't take long.

On the second night following her little to do with Mary Anne, she was sitting at the drugstore counter sipping a coke when someone slipped onto the stool alongside her. It was a hot, muggy night, and Charlene felt miserable. She was wondering whether she would be able to sleep at all. Hence, she wasn't at all pleased when she heard a low voice say, "So you're Charlene Duval."

Charlene looked up into a pair of tawny eyes on a level with her own. She let her eyes slide rudely over the figure dressed in a tawny play-suit, noting that the girl was tall, as tall as Charlene herself. She noted the tawny hair. Everything about this girl was tawny, and Charlene. had the instant impression of a leopard, without the spots.

"So you're Karen Brent," she said finally.

The tawny eyes widened a little, then crinkled at the comers as the pink lips smiled. "Well, well, little Mary Anne does talk a lot.,, Charlene said nothing.

"Well," Karen went on at last, "since we apparently know so much about each other there's no sense in wasting a lot of time, is there."

Charlene still said nothing.

"Oh, I get it. Okay, Strong and Silent, I'll put it straight. I came in here to invite you for a moonlight swim. I looked you over earlier, and came to the conclusion you might be interesting to — er — meet." Then the tone took on a sneer. "Especially since I've heard so much about you."

Charlene looked at her again, expressionlessly. "Nasty little bitch, aren't you." her eyes widened again, then narrowed. "Watch it, butch. You could get into trouble like that."

"Blow," was Charlene's succinct advice.

The girl tensed, one hand half-raised like a claw. Then her eyes went to the other people in the place, and she relaxed again. She looked Charlene over more carefully. When she spoke again her tone was entirely different. "Hey, you might really be interesting, at that. Why don't we start all over again?"

Charlene returned the inspection. "Okay, why don't we?" ·

"Fine. I'm Karen Brent and I'm glad to make your acquaintance and I'm inviting you to a moonlight swim in Mary Anne's, well, semi-private, at least, lake. Mary Anne need know nothing about it. I won't tell her, and I can tell from your attitude that you sure as hell won't. I've got everything we'll need in the car, and I know a way back to the lake that won't take us near Mary Anne's house. Besides, it's shorter than the way from the house. There's a nice full moon tonight, so we won't fall into any hidden traps or sinkholes." She stopped, moved her lips silently, counting on her fingers. "I guess that covers it." She turned on the smile again. "How about it, Charlene?"

Charlene returned the smile. "I guess you covered almost everything. I'll have to go for my suit, though."

Karen's smile was lightly mocking. "Suit?"

"My error." Charlene put down a dime for her coke, slid off the stool. "Lead on, MacDuff." In less than five minutes Karen pulled well off the road, parking behind a mass of shrubbery which hid the car from the highway. She pulled a blanket out of the back seat, waved a hand. "Off to the wilderness."

As they moved across the uneven surface of a field Karen began to complain about the footing, then about the town and the people. By the time they entered the edge of the wooded area she was complaining about everything under the sun, while Charlene listened in silence. The nasty tone was back in Karen's voice, and Charlene decided that the girl was a completely spoiled brat, used to having her own way in everything except getting out of such a dead town populated by such stupid people. She probably got her only joy in life out of her domination of Mary Anne Adams.

At the lake Karen threw the blanket down petulantly and tore the play-suit away from her body as if she wanted to destroy it. Then she turned, posing for Charlene in the bright moonlight. But Charlene was busy undressing, not even looking at her. This was too much. "Dammit, Charlene, you came out here with me; you might at least look at me."

Charlene paid not the slightest attention to her until she had completed her own undressing. Then she looked long and steadily at the gleaming figure, turned and ran toward the lake. She heard Karen's muttered curse behind her, and her faint smile showed itself. She heard Karen splashing toward her, deliberately kept her back turned. She felt Karen's arms come round her, the hands reaching and sliding. She thrust the girl away with a bump of her rear, and disappeared in a surface dive. Surfacing again, near the shore, she casually walked to the blanket and dropped down on it. She watched Karen's glistening body leave the water and trudge angrily toward her. She wiped the smile off her face and closed her eyes. Charlene heard Karen's angry breathing above her. Then, Karen's angry voice: "What the hell's wrong with you, Charlene? If you're so bored, why in hell did you come out here in the first place?"

Charlene opened her eyes. "Take it easy, Karen. What's the rush?"

Karen flopped down beside her, lay quietly for a minute. Then her hands began to creep. Charlene grabbed them and held them down. "Easy, I said."

Karen snorted disgustedly. "H ll, I might as well have gone to bed early tonight — alone. And Mary Anne said you were so great... "

"Kindly shut up about Mary Anne, Karen."

Karen gasped. "Who the hell do you think you are?"

Charlene sighed, rolled away from the girl, trying to shut out the complaints that followed the short silence brought on by the sharp words between them. Eventually, while Karen went on, Charlene rose nonchalantly to her feet stood over the supine figure of the complainer, and planted the sole of her left foot on the girl's mouth, bringing a sudden and complete halt to the conversation.

"You talk too much, Karen. Like Mary Anne, but you're much less interesting."

Karen stared up at her, wide-eyed with shock. Then her hands gripped Charlene's ankle and wrenched the foot from her mouth. "*Goddamn* you ... " She twisted the ankle, throwing Charlene off balance. Then she was on her feet, aiming a clawed hand at Charlene's face. But Charlene had her balance back, and she was much quicker than Karen. She caught the flashing hand, forced it down and back behind the girl. Her other arm went round Karen and caught the same hand. Her arms tightened, pinning Karen tightly against the front of her body, her two hands forcing the captive arm up sharply behind the girl's back, bringing a gasp of pain from Karen's lips.
"Don't try that again, Karen. I'll break you in two."

Karen snarled, again reminding Charlene of the spotless leopard, and her head came forward and down, her teeth reaching for Charlene's shoulder. But again Charlene moved faster. She dropped her shoulder, driving it up under Karen's chin, forcing the girl's head back painfully; at the same time she gave an upward push on Karen's trapped arm, bringing a shriek of pain. She felt Karen's body sag against hers. She held the girl that way for a few seconds, until she felt her own rage abate somewhat. She smiled wolfishly. "Like to bite, eh. That can work two ways, dear."

She let go the grip of her left hand on Karen's wrist, brought the hand around to cup the up-tilted chin and hold it in place while she dropped her shoulder from its wedged position. She opened her mouth wide, pressed it against the slender throat, catching the girl's windpipe between her teeth. Then she closed down on it, slowly tightening the bite until she heard Karen's breath come in slow whistling sounds. The straining body weakened little by little against her.

When she felt it beginning to sag limply she released the grip of her teeth, at the same time dropping the arm that had been twisted behind the girl's back. Karen staggered, caught her balance. Her hands came up to rub her throat, while her shocked, fear filled eyes stared at Charlene's expressionless face. Her whisper was husky and awed. "Good God — "

"Don't bring God into this, Karen. You're dealing with *me*."

Karen stared at her in silence, mouth open, still rubbing her throat. Charlene smiled suddenly, her hands coming up to reach out toward Karen. And Karen cringed backward, like a trapped animal. Charlene chuckled, and Karen shivered violently.

"Come on, Karen. I'm not going to hurt you." Charlene reached again, pulled Karen's hands down to her sides. Her own began to massage the tender flesh of Karen's throat. "You're supposed to be the teacher, according to rumor, but you've got a lot to learn yourself." Her hands rested lightly on Karen's shoulders, but her whisper was sharp. "Kneel, Karen."

"Wha —what?"

Charlene's hands tightened. "You heard me. Do it." Karen knelt, her eyes still wide and locked on Charlene's. Charlene dropped her feet toward Karen's kneeling figure. "You objected to my foot,

Karen. Now you'll get used to it." She raised her right foot and began to move it slowly over the girl's body. She skimmed the shoulders, moved to the abdomen, along the thighs. She smiled into Karen's wide eyes, noting the slowly changing expression in them. At last she moved the foot upward and pressed it softly against Karen's lips.

"There. We're back where we started." She held the foot still. Then: "What are you waiting for, Karen? You know what I want. Do it."

Karen hesitated. Then her lips formed a kiss on the sole of Charlene's foot. As if that had broken the ice, her hands came up to hold the slim ankle, and her lips kissed again, more convincingly this time. She started to move from her kneeling position, but Charlene's voice stopped her. "No." Karen froze and Charlene pulled her foot from the girl's hands, running the big toe lightly down the front of Karen's body. She finally held the foot steady and began a little wiggling movement of the toe alone. She felt Karen's body stiffen and then begin to tremble.

She dropped her foot to the blanket. "Come up here, teacher." Her hands beckoned, and Karen moved forward, still on her knees, until she was astride Charlene's waist. Charlene's hands stopped her there, rising to cup the impudently thrusting breasts. She juggled them a few times as if testing the weight and solidity of two grapefruits in a market. Then her fingers tightened, tugging. "Come teach me, teacher. Let's see how good you are."

Karen came down from her crouch until her lips were against Charlene's. She began to teach, and Charlene was forced to admit that the girl was an excellent instructor. When the wave came for Charlene this time, it was higher, warmer, and immeasurably more violent in its tossing than it had been with Mary Anne. Mixed with the purely physical sensation was the sweetness of the knowledge that she could have anything she wanted from Karen. The girl was her slave, literally, and Charlene gloried in her new found power.

But, unfortunately, her glorying was a little premature. She found it out the very next night, when Karen approached her as she was leaving the theater. Karen was all smiles, all eager with submissive gladness to see her again. She positively wriggled as she stopped Charlene almost apologetically.

"Darling, are you free tonight? I — I mean, if you are, I'd like to have you come with me to a party." "I'm sorry, Karen, but I don't feel like swimming tonight."

"No, no. I don't mean that. I mean a real party, with other people there. We can dance and drink and have a real ball." She was so aglow and at the same time shy about it that Charlene warmed to the idea.

"To listen to you, it'll be a real wingding."

"Oh, it will. Believe me it will. You'll love it. Please come, darling. I'll have a lot more fun with you there. Please?"

Charlene laughed. "Okay, Karen, you sold me. But I'll have to go change clothes first."

"Let it go. Nobody will be dressed up for this. It's in a cabin, anyway, about five miles from town, on the river. Come on, I've got the car right here. Let's go! She caught Charlene's hand tugging eagerly. Charlene laughed again and let herself be dragged along. The leopard was more like a playful kitten tonight. Charlene felt a flash of smug satisfaction at the spoiled Karen's obvious enthusiasm for her company.

Charlene started to climb into the car, then paused in surprise as she caught sight of another woman, in the back seat. Karen laughed lightly and introduced the stranger as "Billie." Charlene stuck out her hand, and then blinked a little as she felt the strength of the other's grip.

And with that they were under way, with Karen explaining that Billie was another guest for the projected party. They swung off the highway, following a dirt road for about a mile. Then they stopped in front of a low, rustic cabin, brightly lighted and with loud music coming from the inside. "Looks as if we're none too early." Karen jumped out. "Come on, before all the goodies are gone."

Charlene followed more slowly, looking down at her uniform in the light from the window of the cabin. She hoped nobody would mind. Then she thought to hell with it. They were probably all girls like herself and Karen anyway. And Billie. Charlene looked at the stranger as she brushed past, headed for the cabin. The woman was short and wide, but she moved as gracefully as a ballet dancer. A powerhouse, Charlene decided. Then she felt Karen's hand on her arm, urging her toward the lights and music. "Come on slowpoke."

Ahead, Billie had reached the doorway and was waiting for them. As Charlene approached, followed closely by Karen, Billie opened the door. At that precise moment Karen gasped suddenly behind Charlene. Charlene turned to see what the trouble was, but Karen giggled and said she thought she'd stepped on something wiggly. Charlene turned back toward the open door just in time to catch a well timed right hook to the chin from the stocky Billie. Her knees buckled and her head spun sickeningly. She felt herself seized from both sides and dragged forward, heard the door close and the lock click. She heard Billie growl, "Tum that damned radio down. Better yet, tum it off." A switch clicked, and there was dead silence, while Billie continued to drag Charlene forward. Charlene's head stopped spinning enough for her to make an effort to stand by herself, but another right hand whistled to a landing on her chin, and this time she blacked out.

She came back to consciousness, flat on her back, under the touch of a cool cloth being applied gently to her bruised chin. She started an instinctive withdrawal, and thus found that her feet were fastened down somehow. She started to brush at the hand with the cloth, thus learning that her hands were under her supine body, fastened together with something soft and slick, but unyielding. She looked up into the smiling eyes of Billie. "Take it easy, honey, those are my ties, and they're plenty strong. Don't get huffy and you won't get bruised — any more."

The gentle hand was still patting her chin with the cloth. Charlene made a sudden lunge for the hand with her teeth, as Karen had done to her the night before. But Billie was fast as well as strong. Her left hand clamped around Char lene's throat, while the right continued its patting of her chin. "Ah ah, little butch. Play rough, and you get hurt. You're not messing with Karen now, sweetie." The hand on her throat tightened almost casually, but Charlene felt her eyes start from her head. The power in that hand was incredible. The grip loosened and the hand dropped away, but Charlene knew better than to move again. She heard a laugh and glanced down toward her feet. There she saw the iron foot-board of a double bed, to which her feet were fastened, and leaning over it, elbows on the foot-board, chin in cupped hands, was Karen. "How does it feel, All masterful? Still feel like a big shot?" Charlene didn't answer as she realized that she had been stripped completely nude and was tied to the bed.

Billie spoke again. "Karen tells me that you consider yourself quite the butch, honey. That right?" Charlene ignored the question. Billie tossed the cloth aside and closed her hands on Charlene's breasts, possessively. "Feel more like a femme to me, honey. We'll have to find out." She took her hands away and nodded to Karen. Then she tangled her left hand in Charlene's hair, not painfully, but firmly, and Charlene recognized the implied threat.

Karen bent to pick up a long turkey feather from the floor. She smiled engagingly at Charlene. "This'll tickle you to death, darling." She sank down on the bed, opposite Billie, leaned over Charlene and drew the feather slowly across her lips. Charlene shuddered, and bit her lips, rolling them between her teeth to kill the unbearably weird feeling that shot through them.

"Isn't it yummy, darling?" Karen did it again. This time Charlene couldn't restrain the chittering moan that burst from her, and her teeth were almost savage in their effort to offset the hellish sensation.

"Karen baby, you'd better stop that mouth bit. You don't want to drive her nuts right off the bat, do you?" Billie interjected.

The leopard was back, and Karen's smile showed it "Of course not, Billie. I want her to last and last and last . . . " The feather moved across Charlene's neck, and Charlene felt the flesh leap and crawl convulsively under it. Down the center of her chest went the feather, and Charlene's breasts quivered and shook. Karen laughed delightedly. "That's nice, darling. Do it again." The feather trailed up over the same path, and again the breasts responded with long shudders. Karen watched them, wet her lips, and began to draw figure S's around them. Around and around and around, Charlene's body began to feel feverish. She began to shake uncontrollably, and when the very tip of the feather slid up to circle the right nipple, Charlene's head came up from the pillow in a spasmodic reflex.

Billie's hand yanked it down again, and the feather skimmed up and over the left nipple. A cry popped from Charlene's distorted mouth, and Billie had to tighten her grip again. Karen was studying Charlene's breasts with a hungry look. "Mmm. Just right, now." She bent to the left one, closed her mouth over the tip. She drew back again. "Nice and tight." She tried the other. "Perfect." The feather went on and on and on, and Charlene's body became a shuddering, plunging thing. She felt the delicious weakness of helpless submission coursing through her, felt her body surging to meet the next touch of the tormenting feather.

Billie's eyes were watching closely, and she finally released her grip on Charlene's hair. Her hands slipped under Charlene's body and untied her hands. Then, still embracing Charlene, she put her lips on the panting mouth. She smiled against the hotly responding lips when she felt Charlene's hands come up to clutch at her back and pull her tighter down. She raised her head and jerked it toward Karen, who dropped the feather on the bed and quickly got out of her clothes. Then Karen came to replace Billie, and Charlene didn't even notice the difference. Her hands clutched at Karen as they had at Billie, and her ravenous mouth couldn't get enough of Karen's.

Then Billie was back, also nude, and together they gave Charlene a master class. They made her butch; they made her femme. When they got through with her, she wasn't sure of where she was, who she was, or much of anything else. Karen had had enough revenge to satisfy the most demanding. They finally allowed her to collapse in total exhaustion, settling down, one on either side of her, Billie producing covers to draw over the three of them.

The next morning, late, Charlene awoke to the sound of voices and low laughter. She listened, eyes closed. Karen and Billie were discussing her and her excellent performance of the night before. They sounded as if they would like to start all over again. Charlene shivered and sat up on the edge of the bed, watching the two still nude figures with their coffee cups at the small table midway between the bed and the fireplace in the wall of the opposite end of the small cabin.

Karen saw her sit up, picked up a heavy glass ashtray in one hand and a lit cigarette in the other, and walked over to stand in front of the seated Charlene.

"How do you feel this morning, darling?"

Charlene looked up at her with a faint smile. "Worn out."

Karen returned her smile. "You should be. You were magnificent last night."

"Well, I had plenty of incentive."

Karen studied her thoughtfully. "Not mad about anything?"

Charlene glanced over to see Billie watching, grin ning. She shrugged. "Should I be mad? I had my kicks, right along with you two."

Karen smiled. "That's the spirit." She laid her cigarette on the edge of the ashtray, reached down and fondled one of Charlene's breasts, tweaking the nipple, feeling it tighten under her fingers. "Mmm, Nice." She ground out the cigarette, set the ashtray on the bed beside Charlene, bent to Charlene's lips, both hands going to her breasts this time, squeezing intimately. Charlene returned the favor with both hands and lips, while Billie voiced complaints in the background.

Karen finally straightened, her eyes bright and her cheeks pink. "Hey, I could really go for you. Too bad you had to be such a jerk at the beginning."

Charlene smiled again. "Well, live and learn, as the wise man said."
"Yeah, live and learn." Karen bent again to Charlene, then suddenly sat down beside her on the bed, seized her tightly in her arms and laid her back on the bed. Her body moved over Charlene's, and her hands and lips began to move with heated urgency. Charlene submitted docilely for a few moments, returning the caresses as avidly as Karen administered them, then she gave a little embarrassed laugh and pushed Karen away gently. "Darling, don't be so impatient." She nodded at Billie. "We have company." Billie laughed. "Yeah, don't you know it's impolite to engage in games without inviting the company to join in?"

Karen was still looking hungrily down at Charlene. "Well, come on, join in." She started to lower herself to Charlene again, but Charlene's hands came up to her breasts, squeezing fondly and pushing lightly at the same time. "Please, baby. I want you as much as you seem to want me, but we might at least wait until I have some coffee, too. Don't be selfish." Her smile, her fondling hands, and the kiss that she formed with her lips and blew up toward Karen did the trick.

"Okay, darling, you can have your coffee." Karen's eyes got even hungrier. "But then I'm going to have you. Oh, how I'm going to have you." Her hands gave one last tight squeeze to Charlene's breasts, and she turned away.

Charlene sat up beside her, running her hand across her "Yes. Yes. I'd like that. Please ... " she said, kissing Karen's cheek. She picked up the overflowing ashtray, and laughed reprovingly, "Darling, you shouldn't have full ashtrays around the bed. Want to start a fire?" She leered suggestively. "I mean a real one, with real flames." She got up, ashtray in hand, and walked casually toward the fireplace. Behind her, Karen whistled long and low. Charlene laughed, and swung her buttocks obligingly. Billie, too, let out a soft sound of approval, and turned back to her coffee.

At the fireplace, Charlene dumped the ashtray and came back with it toward the bed. She walked close behind Billie, who was

just raising her cup for a sip. Without changing pace or expression, Charlene swung the heavy receptacle against Billie's head,
just above the ear. Billie's cup crashed to the table and her body
slid from the chair with a heavy thud. Charlene didn't even look
at her. Her eyes were fixed on Karen, sitting in complete amazement on the edge of the bed. Then Charlene was standing in
front of her, swinging the ashtray idly at her side.

"Want some of the same, baby?" Charlene's smile was soft and
dreamy.

Karen didn't answer. She couldn't. Her eyes watched the swinging ashtray, watched Charlene's other hand come _up lazily to
wrap around her throat, almost caressingly. She felt the fingers
tighten and push back ward. She let her body go until she was
flat on her back, Charlene's hand still gripping her throat. Then
Charlene dropped the ashtray, put her other hand on Karen's
throat as well, and started squeezing, her knee planted in Kar-
en's stomach. Karen's body began a struggle to save itself, but
Charlene bore down harder. The girl's body finally slumped with
shocking suddenness, and Charlene let go. She watched the
struggle for breath, turned to glance at Billie, who hadn't moved
an inch. She looked down at Karen again, watched the tawny
eyes finally open, and saw the raw fear leap into them. She
smiled again, her dreamy smile. Then her eyes caught sight
of the discarded feather from last night, mixed up in the tangle
of bed clothes. She picked it up, waved it under Karen's nose.
"Maybe you'd like this better?"

Karen's eyes moved to the feather, and her expression changed
slowly to one of infernal hunger. Her body trembled, and her
whisper was almost eerie.

"Yes. Yes, I'd like that . Please ... "

Charlene found herself almost caught in the fever that suddenly
possessed the other girl. She started to put the feather to work,
stopped with a grimace. Damned if she'd cater to Karen's hunger, last night was enough. She dropped the feather, balled her
right fist, and clipped Karen as she herself had been clipped the
night before, making sure it was hard enough.

Karen slumped limply back on the bed, and Charlene turned
to examine her but Billie was too rugged to be damaged much
by one clout on the head. Charlene found her clothes, dressed
leisurely, turned at the door to blow a kiss to the two sleepers,
slammed the door behind her, dusting her hands together as she
started toward the highway. Then she stopped. Why not use the
car standing so conveniently there for her? She found the keys
in the ignition, and in a matter of twenty minutes she was parking
deliberately in a red zone on Main Street.

She sat for a moment, debating with herself as to whether she
should take the keys with her to drop into the first trash can she
came across. She smiled, got out of the car, leaving the keys in
the ignition, slammed the door, patted the front fender of the car,
and started walking toward her rented room. She stopped at the
first public phone booth, called the home of the theater manager,
and, in a sad little voice, asked him if she might get the pay that
was coming to her.

Her dear old aunt was deathly ill, not expected to live and she
had to rush to her bedside. Her lip curled as the manager's voice
assure her that it was perfectly all right, that ·be would have the
money for her whenever she stopped by. She thanked him tear-
fully, hung up, and went on to her room. She packed her things
in her one suitcase, totaled her travelers' checks, and decided
she could spend a couple of hundred on a used car. She wrote
a short note to Curt and "Aunt" Martha, set her bag by the door,
and took off, dropping the note into the nearest mailbox. An hour
later she drove up to the theater manager's. door in an eight-
year-old Chevy two door sedan, thanked him again for the check
he banded her, wiped her eyes furtively, and set out to pick up
her suitcase and explain her sudden departure to her kind old
landlady.

Her whole outer-world experience, thus far, as theater usherette
and lesbian lover, had lasted less than two weeks, but she was
happy with her progress in both areas. She headed for Chicago.
There, she reasoned, she should find all kinds of new experiences and adventures. Every girl, in her opinion, should head for
Chicago at some time or other in her young life.

She cruised happily, enjoying the lazy look of the countryside, until she came upon a sign Hal's Drive In. She remembered she hadn't yet eaten anything, and sudden hunger pangs hit her. Pullin in she looked around while she waited for the carhop to get to her. She noted a sign on one window of the place: Girl Wanted, Experience Preferred. Her eyes moved on to the beginning of a small village just beyond the drive-in and she wondered idly what the people found to do in a place like that.

"Not much of a town, is it?" The voice had a tired smile in it.

Charlene's eyes came back to look into those of the carhop at the side of the car. "No. At least it doesn't look like much." The carhop laughed, a little bitterly, Charlene thought. "It's no more than it looks. Believe me, I know. I live here."

"That must be the reason for the sign." Charlene nodded toward the Girl Wanted plastered to the window of the building.

"That's mainly it. Nobody wants to work in a god forsaken place like this."

"No business?"

"Oh, business is all right. But the nearest town of any size is Kanesville, about seven miles west of here, and even it's nothing. Chicago is at least an hour and a half drive."

Charlene laughed. "Sounds bad. Well, give me a hamburger, with the works, and a cup of coffee. Maybe the food's better than the surroundings."

The carhop grinned. "If it wasn't, this place'd fold in five minutes." She turned away to the service window of the building, and Charlene continued her look around. She decided that the place could challenge the patience of a monk. Real boredom was something Charlene had never experienced, and her eyes grew thoughtful. The carhop came back with her order.

"I suppose you're headed for Chicago?"

Charlene nodded. The girl's face turned wistful. "God, how I wish I could go with you."
"Why can't you?" Charlene was honestly curious.

"I've got to get some money together before I can go anywhere."

Charlene waved a hand. "Hell, I won't charge you anything for the ride."

The girl hesitated. "Yeah, but when I got there, what would I do?"

Charlene shrugged. "You'd find something."

Another hesitation. "Gee, I'd sure like to. But I guess I'll have to stick it out here for a while yet." The girl turned reluctantly away to take an order from a car which had just rolled in. Charlene's eyes followed her musingly. Why were people so willing to be led by circumstances, real or imagined? Why couldn't they make their own circumstances? Her eyes came back to the sign on the window. Then she was out of the car, headed for the service window, where the cashier rode herd on the money.

Ten minutes later, despite her lack of experience, she had a new job. By mid-afternoon, she had found and rented a small cabin well back from the road and comfortably away from the nearest neighbors.

The next morning when she reported for work, dressed in the not too badly fitted uniform furnished by the company, the disgruntled carhop of the previous day looked at her in complete amazement, shook her head. "Gal, you must have rocks in your head."

Now, in her bedroom, watching the paling of the sky and hearing the first twittering of the birds through the open window, Charlene grinned and turned on her side. Yes, Mary Anne had really started a rapid-fire chain of events.
Charlene closed her eyes, slept finally, this time without dreams or disturbance.

3

LAYING PIPE

A few nights later, Charlene was again lying flat on her back on her bed, her eyes turned to the open window, a slight frown on her face. She was thinking again of Cynthia, and the thoughts made her uneasy, as they always did lately when she thought of the tiny girl. Something would have to be done. Heretofore, she had kept her rendez-vous away from her own living quarters, because of some vague sense of propriety or privacy or something. But tonight, her night off, Cynthia's car had driven directly to her cabin and the two of them had dallied and experimented for long, delicious hours. The warm green wave had risen and fallen, risen and fallen, and now the heavy breathing and whispered endearments had faded into silence, leaving Charlene full of wonder and unease.

Cynthia's little hands were cupped under Charlene's shoulders, and she wiggled, settling her warm breasts more snugly against Charlene's. "Darling, are you sure I'm not too heavy for you?" Charlene's hands stopped their stroking of the satiny back and slid down to cup the round buttocks. "Baby, when you get too heavy, I'll let you know. Now you just be quiet. I'm thinking." Cynthia's lips pressed quick little pecking kisses on Charlene's neck, her cheeks, her lips. "I love you, Charley. I love you."

Charlene's hands tightened, then went back to stroking the smooth back. "Yes, baby. I know." There was more silence. Then Charlene sighed deeply, tightened her arms around Cynthia. "Give me a kiss, baby." And when Cynthia obeyed, Charlene's lips bruised hers for a long moment, then Charlene's hand gave her a sharp spat on the fanny, rolled her over on her back on the bed. Charlene's arms squeezed her tightly, and then Charlene rolled away "Okay, baby, it's time to get you out of here."

They dressed in silence, but as they started for the door, Cynthia asked in a small voice, "Won't you at least go with me down to the drive-in for a cup of coffee?" Charlene smiled down at her. "Sure, honey, I'll do that."

Outside, they settled down in Cynthia's car, Charlene on the driver's side. Her hand reached for the switch, but before it got there, something hard caught her just above the right ear, paralyzing her almost completely. A familiar voice came dimly to her ears: "Turn about, little butch." At the same instant her glued eyes caught a glimpse of an arm snaking about Cynthia's throat, pulling her sharply against the back of the seat, and another familiar voice said, "Not a peep, small stuff. One yipe, and you'll regret it '' Then Billie's hands were pulling Charlene almost effortlessly backwards over the seat into the back of the car, and Billie's voice was saying, "Okay, Karen, get behind that wheel. You know where to go."

The car was in motion, Billie's one hand holding Charlene across her lap. Charlene saw Cynthia huddled in the front seat, her eyes wide, and she wondered if the man girl's nipple were tight and distended. Billie was looking down into Charlene's eyes, grinning maliciously. Her hand moved roughly over Charlene's body, and her voice was sneering. "Too bad we have to work over such a dish." Her hand slipped under the old sweatshirt that Charlene had put on when she and Cynthia left the cabin. The blunt fingers closed brutally over one breast, and despite the haze that covered her brain, Charlene felt an agonizing pain shoot through her whole body. She arched against it, a hissing moan escaping between her set teeth.

Billie grinned wider, tightening her grip even more on the soft mound, and her other hand waved a short piece of lead pipe before Charlene's eyes. "Relax, butch, before I give it to you here and now. And I'll tear those tits right off you." Charlene forced herself to relax despite the agony, and Billie let go, nodding her approval. "You learn quick, butch. Before I'm through with you this time, :you'll really be educated." She looked at Karen. "Come on, Karen, get this thing moving. I need some exercise." Her glance shifted to Cynthia, sitting wide-eyed and trembling beside the driver. "You're gonna get a chance to see your 'boyfriend' worked over good, honey. I hope blood and bruises don't bother you too much." Her grin was wolfish. Cynthia looked at it, and her trembling increased. She opened her mouth to say some-thing, but Billie cut her off. "Keep it shut, small fry, and you got nothing to worry about."

Charlene lay quietly across Billie's lap, trying to gather her wits. The roughness of the ride told her that the car was on a dirt road now, and finally it slowed to a stop. Karen turned her head. "Well, here we are. Nobody'll hear anything from here. Let's go" She grinned down into Charlene's upturned face. "Just wait, hon-ey, just wait. We're gonna have a ball tonight." She flicked her open hand across Charlene's face, bringing moisture to Char-lene's eyes from the sting.

Billie's hand fumbled at the back of Charlene's neck, gripping a handful of the top of the sweatshirt, raised her to a sitting po-sition and thrust her toward the door. "Okay, butch, outside." Her hand kept its grip as Charlene fumbled the door open and stumbled out, Billie right behind her. Karen got out and moved to join them, leaving Cynthia huddled in the seat. Then she turned back, took the keys out of the ignition, shook an admonishing finger at Cynthia. "Don't go 'way, honey. We won't be long."

As the three started away from the car, Billie's hand still hold-ing Charlene's sweatshirt collar, Cynthia let out a wailing plea. "Please don't hurt her. Please. Look, I — I've got some money. I'll pay you, but please let her go. Please!" There was derisive laughter from Karen and Billie. Then Karen suddenly stopped laughing, and put a hand on Billie's arm. "What a minute. I've got an idea." She raised her voice. "Come here, kid." She watched Cynthia scramble out of the car and run eagerly toward them. "So you'll pay us to leave her alone, eh? How much?'
W—well, I don't have much with me." Cynthia's voice brightened. "But I can get more. As much as you want."

"Why, baby? You in love with this — this creep?" Cynthia's voice was small, but firm. "Yes, I am." Karen nodded, turned to look at Charlene, who was watching silently. "That right? You two in love, are you?"

Charlene didn't answer right away. Her eyes went to Cynthia, came back to Karen, glanced at Billie. "Yes," she said finally. Karen mulled slowly. "How nice." She looked at Billie, winked, took Cynthia's hand and began to talk to her in clear, specific terms, telling her how she could save Charlene from a great part of the beating they had planned for her. Not all of it, of course, but the greater part of it. The moon was on the wane, but it was still bright enough for all of them to see the fiery blush that crept over Cynthia's face. When Karen stopped talking, the blush was even redder. Cynthia looked at Charlene, and murmured agreement to Karen's conditions.

Karen looked at Charlene with a vicious grin. "You don't mind, do you, lover? It's to save your skin, you know." Billie answered for Charlene, tightening her grip on Charlene's collar. "Naw, she doesn't mind. Wouldn't do her a hell of a lot good if she did. I wanna watch this." She snapped to Charlene, "Down on your back, butch."

Charlene obediently knelt, then lay back on the ground. Billie raised one foot, placed it on Charlene's throat. "Karen didn't dig this when you did it to her. How do you like it?" Charlene didn't waste her breath with an answer that Billie didn't expect anyway. Her eyes watched Karen lead Cynthia up to within a few feet of where she lay. She watched Karen step behind the small girl, her hands coming around to unbutton Cynthia's sweater and slip it back and down the unresisting arms. She watched the white gleam of Cynthia's trembling breasts, watched Karen's hands slip up to cover them, squeeze and roll and flatten them, bounce them lightly in her palms. She watched Karen's fingers twist the erect nipples, press them. Karen looked down at Charlene — "Jealous, lover?"

Cynthia's eyes remained on Charlene's all during this. Her head tilted to one side as Karen's lips came down to glide over her shoulder and up the side of her throat. Her every move was made to enhance Karen's manipulations of her body. Her eyes pleaded with Charlene for understanding.

Charlene watched blankly, gulping occasionally under the light pressure of Billie's foot on her throat. Karen was stripping the skirt and panties away now, her hands probing the tiny body as she worked. Then she stepped back and undressed herself with hurried motions. She stepped forward again, her hands coming around Cynthia to press the girl's nudity back tightly against her own. She'd forgotten Charlene by now, and her hands were eager in their turning of Cynthia's yielding softness so that they were pressed together face to face.

Karen's lips came down on Cynthia's waiting mouth, and, as Cynthia's arms came round her neck in a tight embrace, she uttered a low moan, her hands darting to Cynthia's soft, round buttocks, clutching savagely, bending the pliant body backward and pulling it up and in to her as her lips bruised Cynthia's in a kiss of . pure hungry lust. Then she was lowering the tiny figure to the ground, smothering it under her own, and the two became a tangle of writhing arms, legs, and torsos, and the air was filled with whimpering sounds. Billie stood watching this with shining eyes, until she felt a movement under her right foot. Her hand automatically cocked the lead pipe but then, as her eyes fell to Charlene, she chuckled.

Charlene's eyes were glued to the two entangled forms on the ground, and her body was moving sinuously, as if in response to an invisible lover. Billie's eyes swept over the body at her feet. She licked her lips. She tensed again as she saw Charlene's hands move up toward the foot on her throat.

She cocked the pipe again, waiting for the sudden move she expected. Then she blinked. Charlene's hands were on her ankle, but they were moving caressingly, not trying to remove it or twist it or anything else. They were fondling, sliding to the calf of her leg, squeezing gently, and from Charlene's throat, vibrating through the sole of Billie's shoes, were coming little crooning sounds. Charlene's eyes were wide, staring fixedly at the squirming sight before them, and Billie felt a wave of heat shoot through her. She followed Charlene's gaze to the bobbing heads, the clutching hands, the twisting bodies. Her ears caught the liquid sounds of clinging lips, the almost continuous caressing moans, and the heat wave within her intensified suffocatingly.

She knelt, pipe ready for any move on Charlene's part, removing her foot from Charlene's throat and dropping her left hand down to replace it. Charlene didn't seem to notice the difference. Her hands stroked Billie's arm, her eyes never leaving Cynthia and Karen. Billie waited a moment, suspecting a trick, then swooped down, her hand turning Charlene's face upward, her lips settling on the wet mouth. She closed her lips on Charlene's, darted her tongue into the panting mouth, and felt Charlene's wholehearted response. She felt Charlene's arms circle her neck, pulling her down harder, felt those hands fumble their way to her breasts, hungrily. She heard Charlene's wordless pleas, and her own answering sighs. She drew back, slipped the pipe into the waist-band of her slacks, and caught Charlene's supine body into her arms, lifting it from the ground, her mouth buried in the arched neck. Her hands went to the bottom of the sweatshirt, forced it upward and off over Charlene's head. Then, as Charlene's eyes returned to Cynthia and Karen, Billie's mouth began to ravage her breasts, brutally. And Charlene's body moved to help the ravishment.

Finally, with a deep groan of desperation, Billie bent to the belt of Charlene's slacks. She had to have that body writhing naked-ly against her. Beatings could come later. But right now . . . her hands worked feverishly. The belt came loose, and Billie turned, her head toward Charlene's, to pull the slacks down.

Charlene's stiffened right hand fingertips came up in a vicious jab under Billie's chin, catching her flush in the larynx with all the power in her arm. Billie collapsed across Charlene's an-kles, gagging sickeningly, her hands clawing at her throat, head thrown back in a frantic effort to breathe. Charlene pulled her feet free, stood up, bent down to tum Billie over on her back. She took the piece of pipe from Billie's belt, walked over to the two moving bodies on the ground, reached down and yanked Kar-en's head away from Cynthia, dropping her casually to one side. She picked up Cynthia's clothes and tossed them to her. "Get dressed, Cynthia."

Cynthia stared blindly up at her for a moment. Charlene spoke in a sharp tone. "Get dressed, Cynthia. The show's over." She looked around at the sound of scuffle, only to see Karen, stark naked, running awkwardly away across the field, away from the car, toward empty space. She yelled a ferocious threat after the retreating figure, watched its speed increase, laughed, and turned to Cynthia again. Her voice was gentle. "Come on, baby. Let's get out of here."

Cynthia was crying brokenly, struggling into her clothing. "I — I'm s—sorry, Charley. I — I couldn't help it. It w—was the only thing — "

Charlene patted her on the back. "Hush, honey. I know. You don't owe me any apologies." She helped the girl finish dressing, then slipped an arm around her and led her to the car. She looked back at the still gagging form of Billie, shrugged, and got behind the wheel. Then she got out again, went back to collect Karen's clothes and toss them into the front seat. "We'll scatter these along the road. Give our friend an exercise in imagination when she figures out how to "get home with 'em."

Behind the wheel, Charlene backed the car around, letting the headlights sweep slowly over the territory into which Karen had disappeared. Nothing in sight. She chuckled softly. Karen was probably still running. Either that, or hiding like a rabbit, expecting retribution to pounce on her at any moment, from any direction. The headlight beams crawled over Billie, who was now lying face-down, quiet. Charlene didn't even pause to see if the woman was still breathing. She started back down the dirt road toward the highway. When they reached the main road, Charlene turned to look at Cynthia. "I said you didn't owe me an apology. I'm afraid I owe you one, honey."

"What do you mean?"

"I mean I'm sorry I got you into this mess." She went on to explain, leaving out most of the details, just why Billie and Karen had come looking for her. Cynthia shook her head and stared at Charlene. "I told you that you had a scent of hell about you, Charley. This proves it."

Charlene had passed the turn to her cabin, pulled up to the drive-in front. "We started out for a cup of coffee, and we're going to have it."

Cynthia giggled tremulously. "Nothing bothers you, does it, Charley."

Charlene smiled her little smile. "Not much, honey. Not much."

They drank their coffee in silence, and watched the carhop leave with the cups and tray. Then Charlene turned again to Cynthia. "Feel better now, baby?" Cynthia nodded, but Charlene could see her lips were still trembling. She reached over and patted the small knee, then headed the car back to her cabin. When they arrived, she turned to gather Cynthia into her arms. Her arm bumped something on the seat, and she looked down to see Karen's clothes in the dim light of the dashboard. "Well, well, we forgot to jettison the undies and stuff. 9h, well . . . ".

She brushed them off onto the floor and gathered Cynthia in close against her. "Honey, I want you to go right home now, and forget about those two idiots." The tiny body quivered against her, and her arms tightened. "Now, now. They won't bother you. It's me they're after." Cynthia didn't respond to her chuckle. Charlene tilted the small face up to hers, kissed the warm lips gently. "Go home, honey. And it might be a good idea if you didn't come around for a while. I don't want you mixed up in my troubles."

Cynthia's arms tightened around Charlene's neck. "D-do you think they might come back?"

Charlene tried to calm her. "I doubt it, honey. They should have learned by now to leave well enough alone. But, in case they do, I'll be watching. Don't you worry." Cynthia's lips came up again, and this time her little tongue went into action against Charlene's.

Charlene hugged the girl tightly, and kissed her more fervently. Then she drew back with a little laugh. "Hey, I thought we went through all that for tonight."

"I know, Charley, but that Karen —" Cynthia stopped short, dropped her eyes. Charlene's fingers tilted her chin up again. "I see. I guess I broke things up just at the wrong time, didn't I?"

"Oh no, not really. It's just — just . . . "

Charlene waited, but Cynthia said no more. Finally Charlene opened her door and got out, walking around the car to open the door on Cynthia's side. She leaned in, gathered up Karen's clothes and put them on Cynthia's lap. She glanced into the back seat, where Karen and Billie had lain in wait for her and Cynthia earlier. She saw a small handbag on the seat, picked it up and asked Cynthia if it was hers. No, it wasn't. She dropped it on top of Karen's clothes. "Hold that stuff, honey." She dug into her right hand pants pocket for her door key, then scooped Cynthia up into her arms and carried her toward the cabin, Karen's clothes and all. She fumbled the door open, lowered her burden to the bed inside, sweeping Karen's clothes carelessly to the floor.

Her hands unbuttoned Cynthia's sweater, making lingering detours in which their lips joined. Stripping away the upper garment, she pressed the girl back into a supine position and started on the lower section. Finally she stood upright and began taking off her own clothing. Cynthia's whisper startled her.

"Charley,. did you mean what you told those girls? I — I mean about us being in love?"
Charlene hesitated for a long moment, a frozen statue in the darkness of the room. Then her hands went on with their undressing and she said, "Yes, darling. I meant it."

"Then — then you do love me?"

Charlene's nude body sank to the bed beside her, her lips coming slowly down to Cynthia's. "Yes, baby, I love you. I love you very much." Then there was no time or inclination for more talk.

Four hands and two pairs of lips went into violent action, and this time Charlene made no effort to slow Cynthia down. The tiny body was like an eel trying to escape from a trap, and when

Charlene sank down at the side of the bed, slipping her hands under the soft, eagerly cooperative buttocks and completing what Karen had so involuntarily left unfinished, the little blonde's cries were such that Charlene had to put one hand over her lips to muffle them.

Dawn was beginning to flush the eastern sky when Cynthia finally left, Charlene gazing after her long after the car had disappeared. She finally turned back to the door, striking the heel of her hand violently against the door frame as she went back into the cabin. She stood for another long moment, biting her lower lip, then scooped Karen's clothes up with an angry hand. She opened the purse, counted $120 in small bills, and grinned. She stuffed the money into her pocket, dug out an ID card and a driver's license from the bag. Karen Brent, with an address. She tore up the ID and the license, flushing them down the toilet. A set of keys appeared next, and this time Charlene didn't hesitate.

She stepped outside and threw them as hard as she could out into the empty wilderness behind her cabin. Back inside, she tossed Karen's clothes and purse carelessly into one comer. She got out her suitcase and packed it, folding the uniform from the drive in neatly and leaving it on the bed. She'd learned the habit drive-ins had for firing girls without notice, having first lined up a replacement for the unfortunate, and she had no qualms about leaving suddenly and unannounced. The uniform would be recognized and returned to the owners eventually.

Less than an hour after Cynthia's departure, Charlene was back in her Chevy, not even thinking about the money she had coming from the drive-in for the. past few days work. It didn't amount to much anyway. By sunup, she was driving through Kanesville, her black eyes turning momentarily to the direction of Cynthia's home, then returned to the highway ahead of her. Soon Kanesville was behind her and she was headed west. Just west. Nowhere in particular. Just so it was a good long distance this time. She took her time, stopping here for a day, there for two days, working as counter waitress for a few hours to relieve an understaffed crew in return for a meal. Sometimes she washed dishes. Sometimes she just stopped to look around some especially interesting spot. She always kept her eyes and ears open, almost like a savage from the jungle, come to civilization for the first time.

So it was that she arrived finally in that Mecca of all young people — Hollywood, the never—never land of the dreamers.

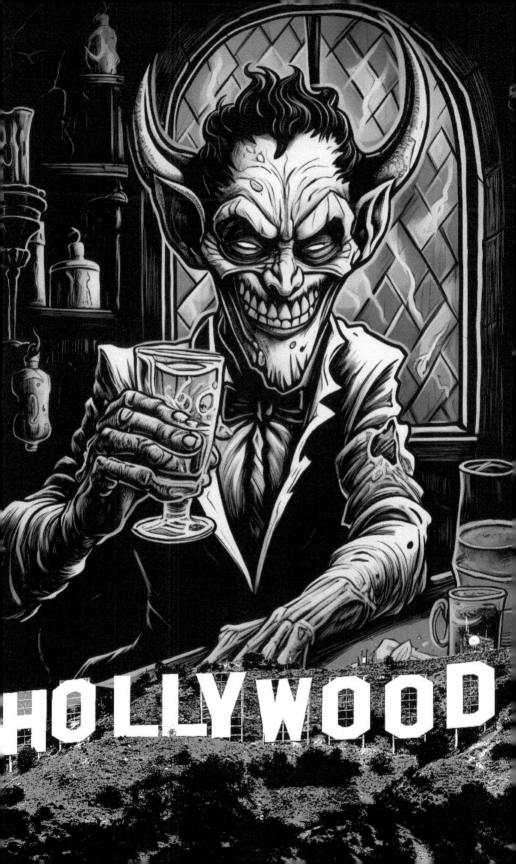

4

JUST ANOTHER NIGHT IN HOLLYWOOD

I t was fall now, and the eternal sunshine of Southern California came down occasionally in drizzles, now and then in liquid sheets. Charlene had been here for several weeks, comfortably ensconced in a job as carhop at Davey's Drive Inn, the ultimate eat-in-car establishment in this territory of ultimates. Lincolns, Cadillacs, and Imperials were liberally sprinkled among the sleek cars that usually decorated the lot.

Charlene's story of her past experience, when she had applied for the job, would have done credit to the most astute of Hollywood press agents. In fact, it would have made the most case-hardened flack blush like a schoolgirl to tell it. Charlene had learned a lot in a short time.
Among other things, she'd learned how to avoid igniting in men that impulse to keep away from her. A little practice with the half-shy, half-mischievous glance, the sweet smile with the eyes down-turned, built her tips into healthy amounts each day. She was surprised at how few actually tried seriously to proposition her outright. When one did, all she had to do was turn that blank stare on him. Unfortunately for her income, such men didn't return to her station after the first experience. For Charlene, how-

ever, the real accomplishment lay in the fact that if she wanted a man she knew how to land one. With women, of course, there was no trouble. She could handle them with boring ease. Most of her tips came from them.

Since her arrival, she'd kept away from individual contacts as much as possible. She'd formed no attachments, either male or female, since her last episode with Billie and Karen — and Cynthia. The thoughts of Cynthia had weakened gradually, however, and she occasionally felt twinges ol attraction for various of the lush beauties that seemed always to be around the place. But she maintained her aloof status. No more complications like that of Billie and Karen, possibly involving an innocent bystander like Cynthia, and yet the thought of Cynthia always sobered her. She wondered how the kid had taken her running away. She hoped Cynthia had forgotten about her by now.

Love was a hell of a thing to get tangled up in. She'd almost exhausted the complete list of things that a girl could enjoy by herself, and she was aware of the building pressure of frustration. The urge to move on again came over her, but she recalled that, as some wise guy had said: "Wherever I go, I go too, and spoil everything."

It was another of those nights when the "sunshine" was coming down in buckets. The lot was completely dead, and Charlene was sitting at one end of the counter, inside, listening to the tale of woe of the diminutive counter girl. Charlene liked the kid. She was faintly reminiscent of Cynthia, but Charlene had not the slightest sexual interest in her. She did get many a laugh from the girl's childlike enthusiasm for the innumerable things she became interested in. Never had she seen a person so much alive and in love with life. She knew that the customers felt the same way about the kid. Her tips were bigger and more frequent than those of the best carhop on the lot, which was saying quite a bit.

She was everybody's favorite child. Charlene herself felt a motherly, or fatherly, as she thought wryly, interest in little Carole McHugh, and right at this moment, that interest was being wrathfully aroused by the tale being told to her by the tearful Carole.

There was this bartender over in Los Angeles, a smooth, suave, man-of-the-world who knew just everybody in the county. Carole had been tickled to death when he singled her out for his attention. Why, he'd park his shiny Cadillac over to one side of the lot and come inside to eat at the counter, just so he could talk with her. He was handsome, he was rich, oh, he was the greatest thing that had ever happened, and he was always so polite! No passes, no crude remarks. Golly!

Then, fortune struck in Carole's mind, when he asked her for a date. She'd been on a cloud for the next 24 hours. She'd primped and fussed and dressed for hours. When he arrived, exactly on time, to pick her up she was in a dither. Would he think she was pretty enough? Had she forgotten anything? Was her lipstick just right? Where would he take her tonight Maybe she'd meet some of those important people he knew!

Well, he'd made some remark about having to go back to his place for something he'd forgotten. He'd invited her to come inside with him while he found whatever it was. Then he'd poured drinks for the two of them, despite Carole's objection that she didn't drink. He'd laughed indulgently and assured her that this wouldn't hurt her a bit. It was creme-de-something-or-other, he'd said. She'd found it delicious. She'd also felt a warm, pleasant, glowing feeling, and she'd laughed harder than ever at his witty sayings.

She'd had another, then another. She'd completely forgotten about the fact that they were supposed to be going out somewhere. She'd kicked off her shoes and they'd danced to soft music from his record machine. He was a marvelous dancer, and she felt like a fairy princess being carried away in the arms of the White Knight.

Then those arms had tightened around her, and the hands had begun to wander. Oh, very softly and delicately, to be sure. But wander they did. She'd pushed them away with a protest. He'd offered her still another drink, but she'd refused, definitely this time. They'd danced some more, and again the hands started their explorations but again she stopped them. A little while later he was beginning to look angry, and his words were no longer clever. They were sharp, then he'd apologize, saying he'd developed a headache. But by now she knew better. What he was trying to do had at last penetrated her hazy mind.

Finally, he'd offered her a funny smelling cigarette, like the one he'd lit for himself which she again refused. She didn't smoke, but she knew what he was offering was no ordinary cigarette. She'd heard of this kind. She was sobering quickly, and she decided she wanted to get out of there. Then he'd become direct in his actions. He'd grabbed her, tearing her best going-out dress beyond repair. He mauled her like a football and told her in no uncertain terms what was going to happen to her before she got out of his hands.

He set out to prove it. He'd hurt her terribly, before she did the only thing she could think of.

She screamed.

And screamed again and again. When he tried desperately to muffle her screams by covering her mouth she bit his hand hard. He let go of her violently, went to the door and threw it open. "All right, bitch. Get the hell out of here."

She'd scrambled for her shoes, crying hysterically, trying to hold her dress together, pulling her coat tight around her. She'd sidled past him, and he'd directed a kick at her, catching her on one hip and putting a big bruise on it. She asked Charlene if she would like to see it? She'd prove she wasn't lying. She'd walked and rode buses to get home again. It took almost two hours, and all the while she was sure that people were staring at her, shaking their heads with distaste for such a sloppy girl.

And that was her romance with the bartender.

The girl started crying again, and Charlene patted her on the back. "Honey, don't take it so much to heart. The world's full of guys like that."

"B—but why did he pick on me?"

"Because you're an innocent baby, and that's what a guy like that is always on the prowl for. Makes him feel more like a man or something, if he can take advantage of a girl like that, like you…"

"A—and he looked so — so nice, too. How can you tell?"

"Honey, I don't know. Experience, I guess. You have to develop a hide like a rhinoceros " She patted the small back again. "It's over now. I hate to sound cynical, but the only thing to do is to forget it."

Carole grinned, a weak attempt. "I g—guess you're right."

"Sure I'm right." Charlene smiled encouragingly. "Remember what they say? In a hundred years … " Then she asked casually, "Where did you say this guy works?"

"Over somewhere in the western part of L.A. I've never seen it, of course, but it must be quite a place." She gave Charlene the name of the bar.

"Well, just stay away from it. You can bet that· he'll never bother you here again."

"Yes, I know." The tears started again, and Carole turned away abruptly and headed for the ladies room. Charlene watched the forlorn little figure disappear into the back of the building.   Then she turned and stared out into the deserted lot, her face expressionless and set.

For the next two nights Charlene watched Carole go through the motions of doing her job. She watched the night manager talk very seriously to Carole a couple of times, an exasperated look on his face. She saw Carole furtively wipe her eyes time after time and try desperately to get back her old buoyancy. But it just wasn't there, despite the kid's efforts.

Charlene's own face settled· into its expressionless mask. On her next night off Charlene walked into a sleazy, rundown joint bearing the name Carole had given her. She saw a small knot of men at the far end of the bar, watching televised boxing and making loud armchair coaching remarks. At the center of the bar, by himself, sat the hunched figure of a middle-aged man, staring into the half empty beer glass before him. The bartender, a slick looking character, in Charlene's opinion, stood with one foot up on a beer cooler, his back against the back-bar. His comments on the fighters were loudest and most authoritative of all.

Charlene took a seat at the front end of the bar, near the door, looking the place over as she waited for the bartender to notice her. The bar ran along the right wall of the fair sized room, while to the right center of the room, against the door baffle wall, stood a garishly lighted jukebox, to the right of that machine, a shuffle-board machine. The floor was sprinkled with sawdust, probably in an attempt to give the place an old-time saloon feel, or per-haps to soak up the drinks spilled by the customers. This crowd looked like the drink-spilling types to Charlene.

There was a sudden cessation of loud voices, and Charlene looked up to see all eyes except those of the solitary beer drinker fixed on her. She saw elbows nudge ribs, and heads bend close together, while leering smiles appeared on unshaven faces. The bartender himself was moving smoothly toward her, a wide professional smile fixed on his face. He wiped the bar unnecessarily in front of her. "Good evening, miss," he said in his best baritone, "what may I get for you this evening?"

"Bourbon and water, please." Charlene responded coldly and dispassionately. The bartender made the highball with flourishes, slid small square red paper onto the bar, and set the glass on it. His eyes looked quizzically at Charlene. "Uh, excuse me, miss, but don't I know you from somewhere?"

Charlene smiled, eyes on her drink. "Possibly, I work at Davey's Drive Inn."

There was a pause. Charlene looked up to see a slight frown on the too handsome face. It disappeared as he caught her glance. "Oh yes. I stop 'in there every now and then. The food is very good there."

"Thank you."
He smiled winningly. "Aren't you a little out of your territory way down here?"

"No, I don't think so." Charlene's eyes were on her glass again. "I came down here to see you."

Another pause, then: "I see."

Charlene smiled coyly at him. "You don't sound very pleased."

"Well, I was just wondering why you should go to all that trouble." Charlene shrugged, took a sip of her drink. "Forget it." She turned to the jukebox. "Anything good on that thing? You know, good." She glanced around the room. "Looks to me like this is a real square joint."

The bartender was studying her. "You don't dig squares, huh?"

Charlene shrugged again. "No time to worry about 'em, man. You know?"

One of the men at the far end of the bar called for another beer, and the bartender turned away, giving her a grin. "I'll be right back." Charlene's eyes followed him, narrowing a little. She leaned forward, rubbing her breasts against the edge of the bar, until she felt the nipples tighten in response to the irritation. Then, as the bartender came back toward her, she made a pro-duction of getting out of her light windbreaker, giving him a close look at the thrust of the bra-less bulges straining under the thin black t-shirt she wore underneath. She could fairly feel his eyes, hell *everyone's* eyes, eating away at her nipples. She got off the stool, tucking the t-shirt deeper under the waistband of the skin-tight black stretch toreadors. Those, with the t-shirt, windbreaker, and spike-heeled, sharp-pointed, patent leather boots, were all she'd worn tonight. She could feel every eye in the place on her now, but her only interest was in the bartender.

She got back onto the stool, tossing the windbreaker over the •ool beside her. "I didn't catch
your name. I'm Charlene Duval."

The man blinked, cleared his throat. "Uh, I'm Jack, Jack Berry."
His smile was a little eager this time. " You say you came down
here to see me? What about?" Charlene glanced quickly at the
men at the far end again, then back to Jack. "Oh, nothing really.
From what I heard about you, I thought maybe ... No. Forget it."

"What have you heard about me? Oh. Our little Carole's done
some blabbing, has she? What did she tell you?"

"Nothing. Not a thing."

The man's face was grim now. "Come on. What'd she say?"
Charlene studied her glass. "Nothing really. I just got the impres-
sion from her that you were quite a swinger. I thought maybe . . .
" She looked around again. "It was just an idea..."
"What was just an idea?"

Charlene looked up at him with a little smile. "Well, you know, a
gal gets bored with the same old routine. Real swingers are hard
to find, regardless of what you hear. Most of 'em all talk." She
took another sip of her drink. "The Hollywood influence, I guess.
Everybody's an actor, or a producer or...."

"Yeah." He gave her another look. "Excuse me. I've got glasses
to wash." He turned to the small sink, made a pretense of rinsing
glasses, his gaze turning repeatedly to her.

Charlene slid from the stool, stretched indolendy, and headed for
the ladies room." Another dead silence fell over the room, except
for the voice from the television set. When she came out again,
the room was filled with the tension and silence that always fol-
lows when someone everyone is talking about suddenly re-en-
ters a room. Eyes crawled over her in minute examination, and
she gave them the motions they were looking for. The smell of
lust was almost tangible in the air.

When she sat down again, the bartender had already forgotten
his duties. He leaned his elbows on the bar in front of her. "So
you're bored. What exactly did you have in mind?"

"Oh, I don't know. Anything out of the usual rut."

"Did dear, sweet Carole give you the idea that I could furnish something beyond the, eh, usual?."

"Look, why don't you forget Carole? She told me nothing, absolutely nothing."

"You sound like you might be worried about Carole, what she might think or say..."

"Me?" Why in hell should I be worried about her? Ive got my own troubles."

"That's good, because little Carole's gonna have to learn to keep her prissy little mouth shut."

"What the hell. She's only a wide-eyed hayseed. Let it go already."

"It's the hayseeds that cause trouble for us , uh , that is the swingers of the world. They don't know how things are supposed to work"

Charlene looked at him, around the room, back at him. "And I guess you're gonna convince me that you're one of 'em, eh?"

"No, baby, I'm not gonna convince you of anything. But I'll convince little Carole of something."

"Man, you're beginning to bug me. Now give me the big gangster routine."
Jack smiled softly. "Who? Me?"

Charlene said, "Nuts." She got off the stool again, walked over to the shuffleboard table. She put in a dime, noticed that her finges were trembling ever so slightly. She concentrated on her game, and finally quieted down enough to run three strikes in a row. She heard a soft voice say,

"That's very good." She wheeled in surprise. "Oh, I'm sorry, miss.

I didn't mean to startle you."

It was the solitary man from the bar. Charlene smiled at him. "I guess I was too wrapped up in the, er, game." He looked like a man who was starving for companionship, rather than a wolf. On an impulse, Charlene asked, "Would you like to play a game?" His response was as if she had asked if he would like to go to bed with her. "But I'm really not very good at it. You see, I don't often get the chance to play." He blushed and looked away. Charlene had already guessed that he wasn't exactly popular with the other hangers-on in the place.

They played six games, and Charlene saw that he was even worse than he had said. But he was enjoying himself immensely, and trying hard. Charlene let him win four out of the six, trying not to be obvious about it. When she returned to her stool, finally, she told Jack to get the man another beer. Jack looked at her with a questioning sneer, but did as she asked.
When he came back to her, he apologized in an offhand way for the remarks that had driven Charlene to the game in the first place. Then he nodded toward the lone beer drinker. "What're you, the Red Cross or something?"

"Why? Just because I bought him a beer? Hell, he beat me four times on that machine over there. And I'm pretty good at it."

Jack looked at her breasts. "And at other things too, I'll bet."

Charlene took a sip. "Depends."

Jack looked again at the beer drinker. "I don't know why the creep doesn't get wise and stop coming in here."

"What's the matter with him? He got leprosy or something?"

"No, it's not that. He's just an oddball. He knows nothing about nothing. Not about sports. Not about *anything* the rest of the boys talk about. He used to be a college professor or something. All he can talk about is some gibberish the rest of us don't understand. He's a jerk."

Charlene needled him a little. "And you're. interested in what the 'boys' talk about? Women and sports and women and the little wife and family and *more* women? Who'll be the next mayor or president or governor, and why should the bastard be shot before he can take office? Big deal."

Jack looked at her hard, a muscle twitching in his cheek. "Honey, you'd be surprised at what I'm interested in, you don't even know!"

"Uh huh." She replied in a deadpan voice

Suddenly he was leaning toward her, confidentially. "Look, why don't you take off before closing time and then come back to the back door. I'll let you in while I clean up the joint a little, and then we'll go see if we can't find something to relieve that boredom of yours." He grinned at her, a wolfish grin. "You talk big, honey, and you look like just what my little old psychiatrist ordered. How about it? You game?"

Charlene looked still again around the room with a disaffected stare. "Sure. Can't be any worse than sitting here swilling down this slop."

"Don't worry, baby. I may have a few nice surprises for you."

"Uh huh." She said, again with the deadpan non-believing tone.

Jack gave her another hard look, then went back to washing his glasses. After a moment he walked past her to dig a bottle out of the cabinet under the back-bar. He hesitated on the return trip just long enough to let her know that some of the boys knew his wife, and he didn't want them getting ideas about him and this sexy broad in black here. "We'll have plenty of time later." He leered and went back to his glasses. Finally he threw down the towel, glanced at her half-full glass, sneered at the beer drinker and rejoined his buddies at the far end of the bar.

Charlene saw him wave his hand deprecatingly toward her once, then devote his full attention to the inane program that followed the fights. She got up, leaving half her drink on the bar, shrugged into her windbreaker, smiled a goodnight to the lone man, and left the place.

So Jack was married, eh? Charlene wondered where he had taken Carole that night. He probably kept a separate apartment just for such doings. She wondered if she would see the inside of that apartment tonight, and if so, what would result. Sb thought about his remarks concerning Carole, and her face took on its blank look. She'd made a mistake by even mentioning the kid's name. If what she suspected about Jack Berry was correct, she might as well have led Carole by the hand into a den of angry bears.

She drove slowly, her head buzzing with thoughts mainly con- cerned with her stupidity in allowing Carole's name to enter the conversation, or even giving Jack a reason for thinking about Carole at all. His bruised ego would have an excuse now for some action against Carole. From Carole's story, and her own impressions of Jack, she foresaw a scene that didn't appeal to her in the least.

It was 2:15 in the morning and Carlene was at the back door of the bar, scratching lightly on the door panel. She hid a smile as the door opened almost immediately. Jack must have been standing there waiting for her signal.
"Welcome, doll, welcome. Come in and take off your things." His crude leer was showing already. Charlene looked wide-eyed at him, smiled brightly. "That sounds more like it. Maybe you're not a complete drag after all." She took off her windbreaker, dropped it on the bar. Jack grinned at her slid through the bar opening and poured her a water glass full of whiskey from a top brand bottle. "Here, doll, suck on this, while I stock the coolers." He started back through the slot, but Charlene put a hand on one of his.

"Look, Jack, I'll put it straight. I am a little worried about Carole. Do me a favor, huh? Let the kid alone. She's harmless!'

Jack leaned his elbows on the bar, taking her hand in both of his. "You look, baby. You come in here tonight looking for me. You want some fun. Now I'm glad you feel that way. I think a lot of fun for you would be a little fun for me." His grip on her arm tightened. "But don't tell me what to do. If you're hip as you try to make me think you are, you know damned well that a loose mouth is dangerous. I was foolish to get mixed up with Carole Hayseed, but I'm gonna correct that error. I'm gonna have a couple of the boys waltz her around a little. Now how does that grab you?"

Charlene pulled her hand away and reached for a newspaper that was lying on the bar. She shrugged, turned a page idly·. "I'm not gonna make a production of it, if that's what you mean. I just thought … " She shrugged again, irritably. "To hell with it."

Jack shucked her under the chin. "That's my doll. You and me are gonna make out great. Wait and see." He came out from behind the bar, rolling up his sleeves and taking off the fancy red vest he wore. "Gotta load the beer, doll. Don't go 'way."

Charlene's eyes followed him as he disappeared down a narrow corridor and rounded a tum at the end. She turned back to the newspaper, but her eyes didn't see the print. She was seeing a "waltz" scene, with Jack Berry's grinning face in the background. She could hear him clucking with approval as the scene pro-gressed. Her hands were rolled up into white fists on the bar, and her stomach muscles were fluttering.

Jack came back, carrying two beer cases which he planked down on top of the bar, turning back to go for more. Charlene didn't glance at him this time, and he chuckled as he passed her. "Good news tonight?" Charlene's fists turned whiter.

On his next trip, he stopped and moved to stand behind her. Charlene sensed his eyes sweeping up and down her body. Then she felt his breath on her cheek, and his hands came to her waist, squeezing and rubbing lightly. His face moved over her shoulder, his eyes fixed on the paper. "Must be really good, doll. What you readin'?"

Charlene shrugged. "Just a story about some new poisonous spider they've found. Common household spider, they say, but its bite is more venomous than a rattlesnake's."

She was standing between two barstools, bent over the bar, and she felt him move close against her, his hands still massaging her waist. His lips touched her ear. "Worse than a black widow, like you?"

Charlene stood still, the flutter of her stomach getting stronger. Jack seemed to notice it, for his hands moved around to her front. "Hey, that's what I like, an eager broad." He pulled her back tighter against him, swaying slowly back and forth against her buttocks. "Don't get too impatient, doll. I'll be through here in no time." He trailed his wet mouth down the side of her throat, stepped back and patted her fondly on the rear.

Charlene's eyes were staring blankly straight ahead of her when he left for the back room again. Her whole body was trembling now and her teeth were grinding audibly. The "waltz" scene flashed through her mind again, this time with an added, sickening touch. This time, Jack Berry wasn't only grinning in the background, he was very much in the foreground, and he was far too busy to grin. Charlene felt her stomach churn.

Her eyes began to wander over the bar, and her mind was a welter of anxious thoughts, mixed with nausea. Her eyes glimpsed a familiar object lying beside the bottle wells behind the bar, and they lingered for a long moment, finally moving on as Charlene shuddered a little. Then they came back to the object, staring fixedly at it. She heard Jack's returning foot steps,. and her eyes dropped back down to the paper.

Then he was gone again, and Charlene moved quickly behind the bar, grabbing one of the little red paper napkins from the back bar. She wrapped it around the object she wanted, picked the thing up and returned to her spot between the two barstools, slipping her prize under the newspaper, where she kept her right hand on it. By the time Jack returned again, she was feeling a little foolish. What the hell was she thinking, anyway?

Jack heaved the two cases onto the bar, wiped his face with his handkerchief. "Well, that's that. Now to load the damn stuff, sweep up a little, and off we go." He stopped behind her again, and there was a long pause. Then his hands were on her waist again, and his lower body was moving against her. He whispered heatedly into her ear in a tone that she was sure he thought was sexy but was just gross, "Baby, you sure are something to look at, front or rear." His hands moved around to her front again, this time crawling slowly upward.

Charlene made no move, and the hands finally closed on her breasts, tightening brutally. His breath came out in a rush against her cheek and neck, and then his mouth was mauling her throat, while the fingers clamped tighter over her breasts. The hands moved down again to pull her t-shirt out of the waistband of her toreadors, forcing it upward and tucking it under her arms. Then the fingers returned to the bare thrust of her breasts, tightening viciously. His hips increased their pressure and movement against her buttocks, and one hand came down to force its way down under the front of her pants, yanking her back roughly against him. He mistook Charlene's hissed intake of breath for passion, and his grip tightened on her even more.

Charlene's own grip had tightened on the object under the newspaper, and when he suddenly slid his hands to her shoulders to tum her, with the hotly whispered words "Jesus, baby, what wild tits — tum around here and let me at 'em," she turned more than willingly, and her right hand flashed up and under his breastbone in a clean uppercut. Her eyes caught the sheen of perspiration on his face, and saw it increase suddenly to great drops as his hands fell away from her. She watched his eyes lower unbelievingly to the handle of the icepick protruding from his body at a downward angle. She watched his hands begin a fumbling movement toward her again, and she made no move to avoid them. She stood there, naked breasts heaving, her blank eyes watching his every quiver. He turned slightly, his hands moving aimlessly, eyes staring into hers, then sliding away. He tried to take a faltering step, but his knees buckled suddenly. He fell forward, his chin striking the top of the bar with a splintery crash, the handle of the icepick landing on the edge of a barstool at the same time. The pick gave an upward lurch as if driven by an invisible hand, and a deep groan sounded from the man's throat. His body crumpled to the floor, rolled onto its back and lay motionless, the eyes staring straight up at the ceiling.

Charlene hadn't moved a muscle. Her eyes watched the body on the floor, waiting for some sign of life. Nothing happened. Eyes still on him, she pulled down her t-shirt, tucked it into the waistband of her pants. She put on her windbreaker. She noted that her right hand still held the bar napkin, and she stuck it onto her windbreaker pocket. She looked quickly around the place, ignored the untouched glass on the bar, pulled out the napkin again and used it on the handle of the rear door to let herself out. She stopped in the doorway for a final glance at the sprawled man. He hadn't moved; his eyes were still staring at the ceiling. Charlene looked down to meet the stare but in her mind's eyes all she saw was a little pile of unmoving "little nuisances". She checked the action of the spring latch on the door, whispered, "So long, creep" and stepped out, closing the door firmly behind her.

She walked casually and unhesitatingly down the alley behind the bar to the next cross street, walked diagonally across that street to her parked car, got in and kicked over the motor, letting it warm up before starting out. She felt perfectly calm and relaxed. When she did get underway, she drove easily, stopping once for a cup of coffee before going home to bed.
She had no trouble whatsoever in going to sleep, but when she did her body began to twist restlessly in the unremembered dream, and the little girl's voice said, ''An' now they're nothin'...''

SATAN WAS A LESBIAN

5

NEW FRIENDS AND NEW FEATHERS

The next day, Charlene stayed in her room. She paced the floor. She sat on the edge of the bed staring out the window, then she paced the floor some more. She started to tum on the radio, then turned away from it abruptly, muttering a curse. By evening she was fit to be tied. The evening and the night were even worse. Two days off in a row could be a hell of a drag sometimes. She thought she'd go completely nuts.

In the early morning of the second day after Jack Berry's unfortunate and premature demise, Charlene threw her bathing suit and a towel into her Chevy and headed for the beach. There she swam furiously and long in icy water under a cold, fog-shrouded sky, until she was blue with cold and her teeth were like white castanets clattering out a wild fandango.

By noon she was home again, this time able to sleep for a few hours. She awoke in plenty of time to get to work, feeling as though she hadn't slept for a week. She was sitting in the employees' lunch room, tugging exasperatedly at the tight black plastic cuffs that decorated her arms from wrist halfway to elbow, leaving bare arm up to where the short sleeve of the form fitting white blouse started. Goddamn Hollywood eye wash. She jabbed the three snap fasteners that held each cuff on, twisting them trying to make them feel comfortable on her arms. She finally gave up in disgust, deciding that it was her nerves more than the cuffs that were bugging her.

She glanced at the clock on the wall. Almost time to start the old, smiling grind for the almighty dollar. She picked up her coffee cup and took the last gulp, just as Carole came bursting through the door, waving a newspaper. "Charlene! Have you seen the papers today!?"

"No, kid, I haven't. Why? What's in them that's so different?"

"Why, that bartender I told you about got killed the other night."

Charlene feigned ignorance. "Bartender?"

"Yes. You know, the one I told you about. The one I had a date with."

"Oh, *that* one. Yeah, what about him?" Got killed, you say?"

"Yes. The police think it was a gang murder. Here, look at the story." Carole was babbling, thrusting the paper excitedly under Charlene's nose. Charlene took an uninterested look at the small headline over the article: "SHADES OF MURDER, INC." She shrugged. "Gee, that's tough, Carole. But you shouldn't feel bad about it."

"I do though. And I've been wondering if I should go to the police and talk to them."

"About what, for God's sake?" Charlene snorted.
"Well — well, I had a date with him just a few nights before and everything. They might want to ask me some questions."

"Honey, if they want to ask you any questions they'll come around looking for you. Leave it alone. Besides, what do you know about Murder, Inc.?"

"Nothing. But what about my date with him?"

"Baby, if they picked up every girl who ever had a date with a guy like he seemed to be, according to your story, they'd pick up half the girls in town. No, honey…" She stopped short at the hurt look that came over Carole's face.

"Now, baby, I didn't mean…" again she stopped short. Then she rose abruptly. "I gotta fly at it." She patted Carole's arm. "Honey, believe me, you'd better just forget it. You can't do any good, and you'd get yourself in an embarrassing spot. Just remember. If they want you, they'll come looking for you. Keep out of it."

She turned away and hurried out, as if eager to get to work. She worked fast and furiously during the two-hour dinner period, her brusque and unsmiling manner bringing more than one frown to the sensitive faces of well-fed customers, and very few tips of any consequence to her cash pocket. The pressure was dangerously high within her now, and she hoped that nobody would give her cause to explode. It built even higher, and she quit caring whether the explosion came or not. In fact, she began to look for an excuse to blow up.

By the time the dinner rush ended, however, she was playing her old game of trying to calm herself by pure strength of will. She was amusing herself by imagining how employees and customers alike would react to her suddenly dropping to all fours and loping around the lot, howling like a maddened coyote. The more she thought about it, the more she felt an attack of giggles coming on, and for a moment was actually tempted to try it. But white coats and straitjackets had never really had much appeal for her, and she tried to think of something else, equally startling but less likely to cause a neighborhood riot.

Suddenly a Lincoln Continental convertible slid into one of the slots at her station. She moved toward it, her mind still occupied with ridiculous ideas to relieve the pressure within her. As she came alongside the driver's door and took at look at the lone occupant, her mind lost all ideas except that brought on by the sight of the sandy-haired, sandy-browed girl dressed in a sandy colored jersey dress with a scoop neckline that revealed the tops of flawless, silken-skinned breasts that reminded her of Cynthia's by their bold thrust and apparent disregard for gravity.

She was reminded too of Karen, in that where everything about Karen suggested the word tawny, everything about this lovely suggested sandy. Everything, that is, except her complexion. That suggested the word silky, from the slopes of the breasts to the hairline. The girl wore no make-up that Charlene could note, her lips were naturally pink, her eyes seemed to change colors as they moved. They were pale blue, pale green, light gray, and suddenly seemed to take on a combination of all three. Whereas earlier Charlene had felt that urge to howl like a coyote, she now nearly succumbed to the urge to emit a wolf whistle. Then, with a slight start, she heard a low, throaty voice ask, "May I have a menu, please?"

Charlene noted that the smooth brow was furrowed in a little questioning frown; then she realized that she had probably been staring like a kid at a candy store. She smiled faintly, looked directly into the light eyes, thinking·"Mmm; all those goodies," spoke politely. "Of course, miss, I'm sorry. I was thinking about something else." She kept her eyes fixed on those of the other girl and let her smile fade away, as she slowly handed over the requested card. The slight frown deepened on the girl's face, and she pulled her eyes away with an obvious effort.

Charlene saw a little shudder agitate the front of the jersey dress, and as he turned away toward the service window her mind was already busy with a plan of attack. The kid in the candy store was going to have her fill of the goodies on display, as well as those not yet visible. The only question was the approach. She busied herself with filling water glasses, glancing out of the comer of her eye from time to time toward the Continental. She saw the girl glance toward her, drop her eyes to the menu only to glance up again almost immediately toward her. Her smile widened and her mind worked faster than ever. As soon as she saw the girl look up and sit tapping the menu on the wheel, she was on her way back to the car.

There, she caught the light eyes with her own while she accepted the offered menu and took the order for a lettuce and tomato salad and a glass of milk. The girl seemed unable to look away, and Charlene felt a surge of triumph. This beauty was hers, and all she had to do was make the victim realize it without a lot of fuss. Charlene didn't feel like taking a lot of time and trouble to ease the girl into a knowledge of the situation. She turned away, letting her eyes slide reluctantly from those of the girl in the car, and she sensed a mingled relief and regret in those eyes as hers left them. Turning in the order Charlene waited impatiently for it to be filled. She put it on a wheel tray and returned to the car, making as great a production as possible out of attaching the tray, leaning much farther than necessary into the car, contriving to force the girl back against the seat to make room for her maneuverings. In the midst of her make-work, she glanced at the girl, only to see the wide eyes fixed staring at her right forearm. She glanced at it herself, then back at the unwinking gaze of the "sandy" girl. She wondered for a moment, then glanced again at her own forearm.

The black plastic cuff? She moved it "accidentally" toward the girl's face, was almost shocked and completely delighted at the reaction. The girl gasped, shrank back, her eyes fixed on the cuff, her lips wet and shining and moving silently. Charlene moved the cuff away again, slowly, and the flushed face moved forward with it, almost as if attached to it. The hypnotized fear of the bird for the snake, thought Charlene. Just to verify her own theory, she moved the cuff again, and again the result was the same. That settled it, so far as Charlene was concerned. The girl didn't know it yet, but she was going to be manipulated like a marionette on a string.

In leaving the car Charlene again turned her unsmiling, burning black gaze on the troubled eyes of the other girl, letting them slide away slowly as she moved away. With her back turned she smiled tightly, feeling a resurgence of the wildness that had filled her before the car had pulled in. But this time it was mixed with the wildness of desire as well. The combination gave rise to a devil-may-care attitude. Charlene was too tense to put everything she had into this situation, and thereby get everything she could out of it She watched unobtrusively, and no sooner had the girl returned fork and glass to the tray than Charlene was on her way to retrieve them and give the marionette's strings another yank. This time, she didn't even glance at the other girl as she undid the tray from the wheel, but she sensed the wide eyes fixed on the black cuff of her right arm as she moved it unnecessarily so that the light glinted and changed on the shiny plastic.

Then, in bringing out the tray, she deliberately edged the cuff toward the intent face, following up until the girl's head was pressed back as far as it could go without bending backward over the seat back. Charlene lowered the arm until the cuff was on a level with the white throat and moved it against the soft flesh. Meanwhile Charlene's gaze dropped pointedly to the unexpectedly full thighs and lush hips outlined beneath the clinging dress. That gaze followed the curves and hollows up over the slim waist and stopped again on the bold thrust of breasts. She heard the rasp of uneven breathing mixed with small vocal sounds as she moved the cuff lightly across the slender throat, she felt the uneven flutter of pulse even through the cuff; and her eyes, still fixed on the unfettered breasts, watched the rise of two sharp points beneath the soft material of the dress. She lowered her arm slowly and openly so that the cuff rested across the upper slopes of the girl's breasts, felt those breasts heave and quiver under the touch.

Charlene looked up to find the pale eyes fixed on her own, and the girl's lips were trembling almost spastically. Keeping her blank gaze on the other's, Charlene whispered, "I'm off at midnight." Then she withdrew the tray, turned her back and walked away as if nothing at all had happened. So intent had she been on her little scene, that only after she had reached the service window did she realize that the girl had overpaid her by three dollars. She smiled faintly, shrugged, and put the extra money in her pocket, not even glancing back to see if the car had left.

It was quarter to twelve and Charlene informed the night manager that she was leaving a few minutes early tonight. Paying no attention to his negative reply, she tossed him her checks and cash, which she had already totaled, and left without waiting for his verification of the take. Five minutes before midnight, sitting in her own car in the street at the edge of the lot, Charlene saw the Continental approach the driveway, slow down while the driver looked toward the lot, then speed up again and pass the drive-in as if the driver were completely uninterested in anything it might have to offer.

Charlene smiled her faint smile and waited. In a few minutes the Continental returned, again hesitated, and this time it pulled onto the lot and into Charlene's station. Charlene started her motor and pulled away without a backward glance. The next day, Charlene went shopping, and that evening when the Continental pulled into her station, she took her time about getting out of it. The wide eyes were questioning and the pink lips looked as if they were uncertain about whether to show anger or apology. Then the throaty voice said simply, "I came back last night."
..
Charlene looked blankly at her. "Something came up."

"Tonight?"

"No, but I'll see you here tomorrow night at eight o'clock" Charlene said it as if it were a foregone conclusion that the girl would be there. She offered a menu, but the sandy head shook slightly, and the girl looked as if she might either cry or scream. Charlene turned away immediately upon the shake of the head, wondering which impulse the girl felt the more strongly.. The next night, Charlene was seated at the counter, over a cup of coffee, when the Continental pulled in. She turned toward it with obvious notice, then turned her back again and deliberately dallied in finishing her coffee. She took her time about pulling her long, light coat about her before heading toward the car. There, she paid no attention to the driver after a short glance,
opened the door and slid onto the seat.

The girl looked at her for a moment in silence, opened her mouth to say something, but gasped instead. Charlene was occupied with pulling on a tight pair of shiny black kid gloves. She was very meticulous in fitting them to her fingers, finally raising her eyes to the bemused face of the girl behind the wheel.

"Where do you live?" she asked casually. The girl told her.

"Anyone home at your place?"

"N—no."

"Good. Let's go."

"B—but ..."

Charlene was paying no attention, her eyes turned to look out the window on her own side of the car. The girl again started to say something, but Charlene raised both hands and smoothed the gloves on them, turning toward the driver to do it. The girl's eyes fell to the gloves, widened, and her hand reached trembingly for the switch. Not a word was said as they rolled smoothly toward the Hollywood Hills. Not even when the girl pulled up outside the garage of a veritable mansion and they walked through the door, and into the house, did either of them speak.

Inside, the girl touched a wall switch, bringing a soft, indirect light to the room, and turned toward Charlene. "May I t-take your — Oh God!" She had made an effort to keep her voice even, but as her eyes fell on Charlene, her teeth closed tightly on the back of one hand and her eyes literally bugged. Charlene had already slipped off her coat and stood there with her faint smile, dressed in her black stretch toreadors, high-heeled, black patent boots, and her latest purchase — along with the gloves — a Russian blouse with an Eisenhower jacket effect at the bottom, of black satin and skin-tight fit. The girl's reaction, in Charlene's opinion, more than repaid the cost of the alterations on the former Russian blouse. She walked casually past the petrified girl, dropped her coat and purse on a chair, after removing from the purse, a small metal tube, which she held in her gloved hand. She turned back and watched the wide eyes as they slowly went over her inch by inch. Then, as she started walking slowly and with a deliberate slinking movement toward her, the girl turned away suddenly with a whimpering sound and almost ran across the room to a console in one comer. She opened the cabinet and fumbled with the mechanism. She stood there, both hands braced on the console, shoulders slumped, her back to Charlene, until Charlene's low voice at her ear mingled with the beginning of music from the set.

"Where's your bedroom?"

The girl straightened with a snap, paused, and pointed a trembling finger. "It—it's — "

"Show me."

Again the girl hesitated, then, making no attempt to look at Charlene, moved off like a robot, Charlene following close behind. They entered a corridor as wide as a room of an average house, and as the girl's hand reached for· the knob of the door, Charlene stopped her with a whispered "Wait."

"No!"

She reached out and slowly pulled downward on the zipper that ran from the back of the girl's neck to just below the waist of the sleekly fitted dress, a light grey this time, and of some expensive silken material, but no less sensational than the jersey she had worn the first night at the drive-in. The girl's back trembled as the zipper pull descended, but otherwise she made no move, her hand still on the doorknob in front of her. She did give one gulping little sob, and said, "Couldn't you at least ... ?" She let it die away, then asked, "W—what's your name?"

Behind her, Charlene whispered with her faint smile, "Does it matter?" It was at this point that Charlene realized she had never gotten the girl's name, but like she had just said; it didn't matter. She put one gloved fingertip against the middle of the girl's upper back and pushed gently. The girl said no more, she turned the knob and stepped into the dark room, her hand reaching unsteadily for a wall switch, bathing the room in soft light from an invisible source. She moved to the center of the room and stood quietly, still not looking back toward Charlene, whose eyes swept the luxury of the bedroom, lingering on the queen-sized bed. Charlene turned back toward the door, moved to close it, then smiled and ignored it. Her eyes fell on a knob beside the light switch, and she fiddled with it, discovering that it was the control of a rheostat which, when turned, brought the light level in the room up to outdoor daylight brilliance. She left the light at that intensity, moved casually about the room, paying no attention to the girl who was standing quietly watching her.

She found a sound system control panel above the head of the bed, turned it up until the music seemed to come from every comer of the room. She moved toward a dressing table which contained various skin creams. She nodded. This chick had no desire or need for make-up. Charlene noted a switch beside the table, similar to the one controlling the room lights. She snapped it on, and a bright light halo surrounded the huge mirror mounted in swivels over the dressing table. She turned the rheostat control, and the light came up to blinding brightness. She put the small metal tube that she had taken from her purse on top of the table, and turned at last to the waiting girl.

The big oddly colored eyes were wide and round, fixed numbly on Charlene, and as Charlene stared silently at her, the girl's head began to move slightly from side to side, in a weak rejection of the unspoken command she read in Charlene's blank gaze. It was as if she knew this was her last chance to save herself from utter destruction, and she was struggling mightily.

Charlene raised her arms slowly, her hands outstretched toward the trembling figure before her, beckoning, but the lovely bead continued its shaking motion, and the quivering lips mouthed silent pleas for mercy. Charlene beckoned again, and when the girl made no move to come forward the black fury in Charlene rose with a rush. Her lips drew back in a feral snarl and her black-gloved hands, still stretched toward the girl, became claws. Her whole body tensed with the urge to kill. On the verge of springing at the girl and grabbing her by the throat, Charlene stopped herself as she saw the curved body seem to slump. The head was still moving negatively, but one foot and then the other moved as if of their own accord, carrying the girl toward her ravisher-to-be. Charlene dropped her arms to her sides, waiting in silence for the girl to reach her. Then, when her victim stopped inches away, Charlene reached up to cup the smooth cheeks in her gloved hands, feeling the girl shudder from head to foot at the touch of the black leather on her face. The wide eyes closed, and the girl stood submissively while Charlene hissed out the last of her rage in a harsh whisper, her hands holding tightly to the defenseless cheeks.

"You're a silly little bitch, aren't you"

The imprisoned head moved slightly in Charlene's grip, and the luscious lips whispered an almost inaudible "Yes . . . " Charlene sensed in that simple word the complete surrender of her latest delicious plaything. She let go her grip on the girl's face, dropped her hands to her sides, and waited for the eyes to open. When they did, she smiled lazily into them and dropped her gaze pointedly to the top of the dress, which was now hanging half-off, half-on the sleek white shoulders. The conquered girl's eyes followed Charlene's glance, and her hands came up in obedience to the demand in the black eyes. She slipped the dress down and let it fall into a circle around her feet. Her hands moved then in an instinctive reflex to protect her bared breasts from probing eyes, and perhaps, even more probing hands.

Charlene's eyes moved up to the girl's face, watched the last brief flicker of resistance die away, then dropped again to the protecting hands still gripping the breasts in a convulsive clasp. She saw the girl's chest heave once and heard the tiniest of sobs. The clutching hands gave one last squeeze and dropped away to reveal two of the most beautiful silken breasts Charlene had ever seen. She studied them thoroughly, unmoving, until the pink tips rose, swelled, and began to pulse. The breasts themselves seemed to swell and tighten under her scrutiny, and the girl's body stirred restlessly.

"W—what are you — "

Charlene's eyes came back to the girl's face suddenly, and it was as if she had slapped the palpitating victim. The words were sliced off as if with a cleaver. Charlene had an idea.

"Where's your dog?"

"D—dog? I—I don't understand."

"Come on. A bitch like you is bound to have a dog. All of you do. Where is it?"

"I - I don't have one. I did, but he died."

"Naturally you kept his collar and chain. What kind was he?"

123

"He was a boxer. Y—yes, I kept the collar and chain. But—but I don't — "

"Get them."

"W—what? *Get* them ... ?"

"Yes, stupid, get them. Get them and bring them here. And *hurry.*"

The girl stood motionless for a moment, staring wonderingly at Charlene, who again felt the surge of murderous rage rising with a rush within her. Then, before Charlene gave way to her fury, the girl turned and walked with the bearing of a sleepwalker toward the bedroom door. Charlene's eyes followed, watching the roll and sway of hips and buttocks encased in black lace panties, followed by the fantastic legs to the high heeled gray suede shoes in which the girl walked with classic grace. Altogether, a morsel to be relished, Charlene thought. Then, as the girl disappeared into the hallway, Charlene moved slowly to the door, frowning thoughtfully. She was wondering about the tremendous rage that seemed to come over her without warning, and without any real cause. She wondered if she might be slipping her mooring lines under the boredom of her current life, coupled with the pressures she'd been conscious of since her killing of that oaf of a bartender.

She leaned against the frame of the bedroom door and watched the sandy girl returning with a black, metal-studded dog collar with chain attached. Her eyes approved the bouncing sway of breasts afforded by this front view, and again dropped to the swaying hips. This was a beautiful animal by any standards. She straightened, blocking the door as the girl reached her, held out her hand wordlessly, and the girl placed the collar and chain in her palm. Charlene smiled approvingly, unhooked the chain and opened the buckle of the collar. Stretching out the collar, she looked at it and then at the white column of the girl's throat.

"Hmmm. Looks about right to me ." She smiled again into the wonder g eyes, held the collar out. "Come, Princess, let's get our nice leash on." She wrapped the collar around the unresisting throat, buckled it, testing the tightness by slipping a gloved finger between the soft throat and the collar. Satisfied, she snapped the chain into its ring. "All right, Princess, down." When the bemused girl didn't move, Charlene gave a sharp downward pull on the leash. "Down, Princess!" She yanked downward again, and the girl sank to her knees under the pressure. "On all fours, Princess. Come on, now, don't be stubborn." She put a hand on the back of the girl's neck, pushed downward until "Princess" obeyed. Then she straightened, tugged on the leash again. "Come, Princess. Let's look in the mirror." Walking backward, watching the wide eyes, she tugged harder, and the girl followed on hands and knees, eyes glued unwillingly on Charlene's face.

Charlene, with the greatest and most satisfying feeling of power she had yet experienced, watched the swing and bounce of the girl's pendant breasts during the trek from door to mirror across the bedroom. She stopped a few feet from the mirror and stepped aside to allow her "pet" an unobstructed view of the two of them, but the girl's eyes followed her movement.

"No, no, Princess. Look in the mirror."

The wide eyes turned obediently, and Charlene saw a start go over the girl's body. The eyes widened still more with what seemed almost a frightened look, then they slowly softened with a luminous glow in them, the pink tongue tip came out to moisten the shining lips, and the eyes followed the chain to Charlene's black gloved hand. They moved from there ·upward to Charlene's face. Under the impact of Charlene's black gaze and smiling lips, the girl's mouth trembled slightly and she made a move as if to rise.

"*No*, Princess!"

The girl I subsided again, with a disappointed little sound, and Charlene knelt beside her, raising her own eyes to the mirror to make sure there was no blocking of vision for either of them. She patted the girl on the head, turning it so that the questioning eyes were directed to the reflection of their contrasting bodies, Charlene's in gleaming black and the other girl's shimmering whitely under the harsh brilliance of the illumination. Then she began stroking the sandy hair, the white shoulders and neck, down along the smooth back and along the ribs.

"Nice Princess," crooned Charlene's voice. "Nice, *sweet* Princess." The girl's body was moving subtly under the stroking, and her eyes, fixed as if hypnotized on the reflection of the black, smooth hands moving over her, alternately widened and half-closed like those of a sleepy jungle cat. But the tension in her body, and the little quivering, in addition to the soft little sounds coming from her throat, told Charlene that she was far from asleep.

On and on went the black-gloved hands, stroking and patting the white buttocks, along and around the full thighs, up to grip the tiny waist, and finally to grip the swinging breasts lightly, then firmly, while Charlene's voice crooned praises to her pet "Princess." As Charlene's hands tightened possessively on the trembling breasts, "Princess" uttered a small sob, and her whole body tightened. Charlene chuckled delightedly, gave the girl a light smack on the buttocks and stood up.

"Princess" started to follow suit, but Charlene's snapped command *"Down"* stopped her. Charlene smiled approval once more, patted her own thighs with her hands. "Here, Princess. Give me your paws." The girl rose to her knees and placed her hands in Charlene's, who took them and squeezed them gently, placed them on her thighs and offered her right hand to the girl. "Give me a nice kiss, Princess."

"Princess" started to press a kiss on the back of the gloved hand, but Charlene stopped her again. "No, no, Princess. Dogs don't kiss like people. Now give me a nice little doggies kiss." Without the slightest hesitation, the girl's head moved forward and the pink tongue came out to lick lightly at the black leather of Charlene's glove. It licked again, and again, and still again. The girl's hands left Charlene's thighs and seized the gloved hand, holding tightly and turning palm, then back, then palm, and the tongue moved faster, covering the shiny black surface with moist "doggie" kisses. The girl unconsciously moved closer to Charlene during this, so that when Charlene finally withdrew the hand with another laugh of approval "Princess" had to throw her head far back to look up into Charlene's eyes, past the interfering jut of Charlene's black-clad, untethered breasts. That jut drew the girl's eyes as if by a physical tug, her hands tightened for a moment on Charlene's thighs, and then started a slow, crawling movement upward, hesitantly, as if fearing a rebuff. But when Charlene continued smiling gently the hands slid faster, clamping at last, tightly and hungrily over their twin targets, while "Princess" pressed her own bare and turbulent breasts against her new master's thighs.

Charlene reached down and turned the sandy head again toward the mirror, and felt the girl's hands tighten on her breasts, while at the same time the eyes widened again and the bare breasts flattened against the slippery black material of Charlene's stretch pants. The girl's upper body, dead white in contrast to the complete black of Charlene's garb, took up a sinuous motion, causing her breasts to move against the sleek material. The mirrored eyes of the kneeling girl shone brighter and her breathing became faster and more ragged. Slowly and with no protest from Charlene, the girl began to rise slowly, still pressing her body against that of Charlene, slipping and sliding upward ong Charlene's slippery, skintight black garments, until she was standing breast to breast with Charlene. Eyes still fixed in the mirror, she slid her arms around

Charlene's neck, thrust her whole body against that of her tormenting lover, and continued her writhing motions, more and more frenetically as Charlene stood unmoving and apparently unconscious of any activity.

Finally, however, Charlene felt the tightening of the girl's body that presaged the high point of emotion. She slipped her arms around the slender waist, moved her hands down inside the waistband of the tiny lace panties and gripped the sleek, tight buttocks in a savage grip, tugging the convulsing body against her with sudden, violent strength. At the same time, her mouth went to the side of the girl's throat, her teeth gripping the taut flesh in a sensuous bite which she held while the body of "Princess" went literally wild against her. She marveled at the strength contained in the threshing body, and she wondered if both she and "Princess ' wouldn't be one solid bruise from painful breast tips to knees. She loved it, and she hated it. She reveled in it, and she was full of contempt for herself and for the other girl. She felt the black fury rising in her again, and, as the straining body finally began to slump weakly in her grip, she suddenly tore the girl away from her, thrusting her down again to her knees with a powerful push on the shoulders. Her fingers tightened painfully on the sleek white shoulders, and she hissed, "Bitch! Don't move."

"Princess" looked up at her in complete shock for a moment, then lowered her head and covered her face with her hands, slumping down to sit on her heels in complete degradation and misery, coupled with the physical release from the high sexual tension that had gripped her so long. Charlene looked down at the bowed figure, her hands clenched into black fists that shook with her efforts at self-control. Her eyes went over the conquered girl, taking in the perfection of the flawless white skin, the voluptuous curve of bowed neck and back, the roundness of the arms and fullness of the thighs. She thought of the swollen fullness of the white breasts mashed against her own, their sensuous and frantic movement against hers. She looked and remembered, and concentrated her whole attention on these things, and eventually she felt the fury leaving her. She felt, instead of fury, her own unsatisfied desire taking control of her. She stepped back a pace and began to tear off her own clothing, dropping it haphazardly on the floor. Nude, she stepped forward again, standing directly over the girl, one foot on either side of the bent knees of her "pet," whose face was still hidden in her hands. She reached down, stroked the sandy hair again, took the girl's chin in her right hand and raised the bowed head.

"Princess" gasped and recoiled slightly at the sudden and unexpected sight of a nude Charlene standing over her, but almost immediately her eyes began to warm and widen as they went over the domineering figure. Charlene let her look for a few moments, then patted her thighs again. "Come, Princess, give me your paws again."

"Princess" looked questioningly at her, and Charlene again patted her thighs. "Come, Princess. Your paws!" The girl hesitantly raised her hands. Charlene grasped them impatiently and placed them flat on her thighs. She again stroked the girl's hair, and slid her hands to the back of the sandy head, pulling forward gently but firmly. "All right, Princess. Give me a nice kiss now." "Princess" started a move as if to rise, but Charlene tugged harder. "No no. Stay right where you are. Come on, now." She gave a sudden sharp pull at the back of the girl's head. "Kiss me, Princess. A nice doggies kiss."

The girl's eyes showed sudden understanding, and her eyes dropped, widened. She hesitated, then, in response to Charlene's urging hand, her head moved forward and she delivered a "nice doggies kiss," followed by another and another, until separate kisses merged into one long, continuous caress. Her arms circled Charlene's thighs in a tight embrace, and her hands clutched at smooth flesh.

Charlene closed her eyes, her hands stroking the sandy hair, the slender neck, and the warm shoulders of the girl at her feet. After a time she opened her eyes, turned them toward the mirror, again studying the lines of her "pet" who was now so enthusiastically showing her devotion. She dropped her eyes to the actual form at her feet, and her fingers tightened possessively in the sandy hair. She felt her body rising of its own accord onto tip— toe, felt it beginning to shudder under the caresses of "Princess." She turned her eyes again to the mirror, watched her fingers tighten more in the sandy hair, watched her breasts tremble under the force of her emotions. Then, slowly, her eyes closed and she felt as if the world had suddenly been swept out into that green sea of hers, out from under her feet, leaving her with no support. Her body flexed, her hands coming down heavily upon the shoulders of the crouched girl, who now looked up from inches away into her face. The wide eyes seemed to transmit a message of abject happiness that their owner had been able to please. The pink, rouge-less lips murmured, "I love you."

Charlene stared blankly for a moment, then straightening up, shakily, gave a harsh laugh. "Love! You idiot! What's love got to do with this?"

The girl's eyes dropped in embarrassed disappointment, but Charlene only laughed again, even more harshly, and reached down to grab the chain which was still fastened to the collar around the girl's neck. "Come on, Princess." Her tone made the word sound like an obscenity. "Come on, it's time to end this stupid business. Come on!" She gave a vicious upward yank on the chain and the girl came gaspingly to her feet. Charlene dragged her over to the bed, pushed her roughly down onto it, and turned away to the dressing table. She picked up the metal tube that she'd placed there earlier, returned to the bed to stare sneeringly down into the wondering eyes of the girl who lay still on her back, completely bewildered.

"Never use make-up, do you?" As Charlene spoke she was busy uncapping the tube and applying a deep purplish shade of lipstick to her mouth. She forced the tube tightly against her lips, literally caking the gooey substance on them.

"N—no, I don't." The bemused eyes were following Charlene's every move.

Charlene smiled down at her with ludicrously smeared lips. "But tonight you do, sweetie. Tonight you do." Capping the lipstick, she tossed it aside, sank to the bed beside the girl, took the sandy head in her hands and pressed her mouth brutally but sensuously to the pink lips, forcing them apart and grinding her own mouth against them. She drew back to check the result, laughed coarsely, and returned her mouth to the other girl's. She drew back again, moved to tear down and away the girl's tiny black panties and remove the gray shoes from the slender, delicate feet. Then she lowered her full length and weight onto the supine body and again mashed her mouth to the other's. She began to move, roughly and violently, her pressing lips stifling the startled protest that the girl had started. Her hands brutalized the helpless body, squeezing the breasts, bruising the hips and buttocks, while her lips continued their painful grinding kiss against the lips now smeared like a great, gaping wound.

Charlene drew back again, her hands going to the girl's breasts, more gently and caressingly this time, while her hips continued their grinding assault on the other's. "Lipstick becomes you, darling," she whispered softly, still with her sneering smile. "You should wear it more often." Her fingers twisting the tender nipples of the girl's breasts in a now light, now tight caress, she returned her mouth to the smeared lips beneath hers.

"Princess" was recovering from her initial shock at Charlene's sudden brutal violence, and her bod yat last began to respond to Charlene's brutal attack. Her arms slid around Charlene's neck, her lips moved in cooperation with Charlene's rough kiss, her tongue carrying on sensuous research in and around the dominating mouth of her "lover." Her hands sought and found the moving fullness of Charlene's breasts, and her fingers returned the caresses that Charlene was showering on her. Soon, however, her hands moved down to grip Charlene's buttocks and drag the assaulting hips tighter down against her, and she loosed a scream of pure delight between Charlene's lips. Her body rose shudderingly, and her fingers clawed senselessly at Charlene's flesh.

When Charlene finally drew back again, lifting herself away from her victim, the girl lay with eyes closed and body apparently boneless, in a state of complete exhaustion. Charlene grinned mirthlessly down at her, reached for the lipstick tube and smeared her mouth again. Then she bent over the supine body and pressed her lips to the white throat, moving them in a dragging trail over and around the smooth surface until it was smeared from ear to shoulder and from chin to collarbones. She smeared her mouth again, closed it over each pink breast tip, turning and twisting her face as she dragged it over the full swellings and down and over the flat stomach. She looked once more at her handiwork, tossed aside the lipstick, sought and found a bathroom, where she cleaned herself up, put her clothes on again and headed for the room containing the console, where the girl had left her purse while she fumbled with the set.

Opening the purse, she gave a low whistle as she pulled out a huge roll of bills. She grinned tightly, picked up her own purse and jacket from the chair where she'd left them earlier. Then she paused. Might as well go all the way. She went back to   the girl's purse, searched until she found a key holder, picked out what could only be the key to the Continental and tossed the rest back. She returned to the bedroom to find the sandy girl still supine, eyes still closed, looking like a white Indian in drunkenly applied warpaint, or perhaps the victim of a particularly brutal axe murder. She spoke sharply, causing the girl's eyes to open with a snap. She waved the roll of bills. "I'm keeping this — for services rendered." Then, as the eyes started to close again, with no sign of protest from the girl, Charlene waved the key. "You'll find the car at the drive-in." Again there was no reply, but Charlene could see tears on the white cheeks. She laughed and said, "Don't forget to look in the mirror when you get up."

She closed the door quietly as she left the house.

6

AND THEN
THERE WAS...

In the weeks that followed Charlene felt her self confidence slipping to an alarming extent. She had expected her little session with "Princess" to relieve the internal pressures of boredom and thoughts about her killing of the bartender, but she found no such relief. On the contrary, the destructive feelings increased to the point where her teeth were constantly on edge. She became even more of a lone wolf than she had been, avoiding people, both acquaintances and strangers, almost completely. She even had little or no time for the petite counter girl, Carole, who seemed gradually to be recovering her former buoyancy and bounce. Fortunately for the kid, thought Charlene, the police had not bothered her at all. Had they done so, Charlene was positive that Carole would never have forgotten it, especially after her blind adoration of that creep.

One thing had happened during the period that drove Charlene into a blind rage for hours, until her cynical sense of humor took over and convinced her that she was really far gone. Why in hell should just another example of Hollywood eyewash get to her so much, she wondered. Was it just because it happened at a time when she was supposed to be off work? No matter. What did matter was the fact of the rage. It worried her. The episode that was so magnified in her mind for a little while was her being called in to pose, along with the rest of the crew, for a series of pictures to accompany a Sunday newspaper article on the drive in, "another of Hollywood's fabulous (and other banal adjectives) successes." Without trying to conceal her contempt, she watched the newsmen flag down impressive looking cars on the street and wheedle the drivers into allowing their vehicles to be arranged here and there, just right for the camera angles, on the lot. She joined the other carhops in "enthusiastically" carrying trays loaded with various dishes to these planted customers. She joined in a group shot of the "happy, smiling, extremely "competent" waitresses and carhops.

She thought of the drooling yokels hunched adoringly over their Sunday papers, gaping with awe at the grand establishment in which she worked. *My! Romantic and magic Hollywood! Why, Davey's is almost as impressive as that starlet who just discarded her eighth husband and celebrated by getting drunk and crashing her car into a newsboy's bicycle. Gee, it must be great to be so important and not have to pay attention to what anybody else thinks!*

Hollywood! Nuts!

Not the least of the things that contributed to Charlene's turmoil was the fact that she had discovered a conscience within herself. The memory of the bartender bothered her more than she had anticipated, despite her feeling that she had probably saved poor little Carole from a completely humiliating, degrading, and no doubt physically painful experience. The thought of humiliation and degradation, in turn, reminded her of the tears on the cheeks of "Princess" as she had left the bedroom. That bothered her too. Just to quiet her own internal fury, she had debased a girl whom she didn't even know, and didn't have any interest in knowing. The ironic part of it was that no furies were appeased. They were, if anything, increased by her stupid actions. She thought back to a million and one items of conduct on her part. Each one now seemed based on her own self-centered desire to prove something to herself. She even wondered about her affair with Cynthia. Did she really love the girl or not?

Probably not. More egotism and desire to prove something in desperation, she thought more than once of going to the police with the truth about the bartender, but shrugged it off irritably.

Let them think the "mob" had done it. They probably would have done the job eventually anyway. The guy had been a natural murder bait.

The sandy girl, however, was another story. Charlene wondered how she might be able to make up for her mistreatment of the girl, but she didn't have any idea of the girl's name, and she was positive she could never find her way back to the mansion in the hills above Hollywood. Needless to say, the Continental never returned to the drive-in, during Charlene's shift at least.

Well, she soothed herself at last, the girl had enjoyed herself during the session, degradation or no. Her self-defense mechanisms conjured up all kinds of excuses for her, but her better sense always recognized the rationalizations for what they were, and self contempt increased her turmoil. She was sitting at the counter one slow night, her sense deaf, dumb, and blind to the goings-on about her, her eyes turned blindly toward her station outside, when a dusty car pulled up and stopped with a jolt just short of running up onto the concrete apron where the service window opened out onto the lot. Charlene's eyes were fixed on the spot, but she didn't even see the car for a few moments. When she did, her first thought was that it seemed out of place here. It was not a Continental, a Buick, a Caddy, or any of the other fancy jobs so common here.

And the dust! Some clods, no doubt, who didn't know what kind of place he had driven into. Her eyes finally moved absently toward the driver and blinked unbelievingly. They moved back to the car, looking carefully at it this time. Then they went to the driver again, only to see the driver staring back at her. Her heart seemed to stop, and she had sudden difficulty breathing.

Cynthia!

With a quick lunge, Charlene was out the door and heading at a dead run for the side of the car. She gripped the window ledge with tense fingers, nearly stuttering under the rush of emotion overwhelming her. "Cynthia! My God, Cynthia, what are you doing here? How did you find me?"
The girl looking back at her seemed to have aged by years in-

stead of months. Her face was dead white, gaunt, her eyes had purple shadows under them. Her lips were trembling, and there was a twitch at one corner of her mouth. Her hands gripped the steering wheel in a tight clutch that showed the tendons of her slim fingers. She looked as if she were on the verge of collapse. She made an attempt to smile.

"Hello, Charley." Charlene caught the exhausted weakness in the voice, and her eyes took in the ravaged face, the tense arms and hands. Her own problems were forgotten in the rush of sympathy that hit her.

"Cynthia, baby, you look terrible! What's happened to you?" Again came Cynthia's ghastly smile. "It's a long story, Charley." Her smile faltered, disappeared, and her face sank suddenly down onto the wheel, between her hands. A wrenching sob came from her throat, followed by shuddering moans of pure agony, and tears streamed, dripping from her lowered face to the lap of her rumpled skirt. Charlene looked at her in shocked silence for a moment, then without even thinking of checks, money, her coat, or anything else, she opened the door and eased the sobbing Cynthia out from under the wheel and took her place.

She started the motor and roared out of the lot without a backward glance. She drove furiously, looking for a quiet street on which to pull up and park, and try to find out what devils were driving Cynthia so as to reduce her to a sobbing, shuddering wreck. She put her hand on Cynthia's thigh in a reassuring squeeze, but the girl didn't seem to notice the pressure. Her sobs had taken on a strangled sound by now, and Charlene cringed inwardly as her imagination painted all sorts of weird and terrible pictures of possible causes for such misery. She said nothing, however, her black eyes alternating from Cynthia's bowed bead to the shadowed streets until she spotted an isolated stretch along a seemingly deserted street. Her eyes caught the word "Nardis" on a street sign at an intersection and finally she swung to the curb, doused the lights and cut the motor, and turned to the sobbing girl beside her, drawing the wretched figure into her arms gently and softly, crooning soothing little sounds as she might a terrified child.

"Baby, baby, don't. You're all right now, darling. Please, honey. It's all right. Charley's here, and every thing's all right now." Her arms cradled the tiny body and her hands smoothed the blonde hair, while Cynthia's tears soaked the front of her blouse. She held the small girl almost fiercely, trying to absorb some of the pain into herself in order to relieve Cynthia's suffering. She felt as big as the world, and at the same time as helpless as a crippled mouse, and, unknown to her, tears formed in her eyes and trembled on her lower lids. She was too concerned with Cynthia to notice and marvel at her own ability to cry.

Finally, inevitably, the harsh, driving sobs softened, then ceased, and the small body made an effort to straighten up somewhat. Charlene loosened her grip, and the tangled mop of blonde hair moved back, to give way to two enormous blue eyes, so filled with hopeless misery that Charlene caught her breath.

"Cynthia, honey, please tell me what happened. What in God's name brought on all this?"

A small white hand came up to touch Charlene's cheek in a hesitant caress, followed by a sudden lunge from Cynthia, and Charlene's lips felt as if they had been brushed by a blowtorch as Cynthia's starving mouth took possession. Cynthia's lips twisted and turned, grinding themselves against Charlene's. They kissed, nibbled, and tried to talk all at the same time, and again Charlene's arms gripped the girl's body, this time in a fiery response aroused by the burning caresses of Cynthia's mobile mouth.

The burning was suddenly chilled to an icy sensation, however, when Cynthia again drew back and looked up into Charlene's eyes, hesitated a second, then said, "Charley, I killed them. I killed Karen and Billie. Both of them. I killed them with a carving knife." Her voice was empty, and her eyes had again taken on the look of utter misery that had momentarily been replaced by the sudden up-rush of passion as she kissed Charlene.

Charlene doubted her ears. She gripped Cynthia's shoulders in bruising hands and her black eyes were wide as she hissed, "What? You what?" Cynthia nodded slightly, her eyes unchanging. "I did, Charley. I killed both of them. They ... they ... " She suddenly collapsed into Charlene's arms as a new cyclone of emotions struck her, and it was as if she began, only to let it all go at once. Charlene, however, wasted no thought on sympathy this time. She forced the girl back, and slapped her sharply on one cheek, then on the other.

"Stop it, Cynthia. Snap out of it. Tell me what happened!" She shook the small body violently. "Tell me, damn it! What happened?"

Cynthia stopped sobbing, gulped once. She seemed unaware of Charlene's harsh measures with her. Charlene drew the girl's head down to her shoulder, her right arm around the trembling figure.

"Now tell me about it, Cynthia. Tell me exactly what happened."

Cynthia said nothing for a moment, staring forward through the windshield of the car and along the straight empty street ahead of them. When she did speak, her words surprised Charlene. "Charley, it's just like that second night, isn't it." Charlene glanced at her, followed her gaze out through the windshield. "Just like what? What are you talking about?"

Cynthia giggled nervously. "I mean . . You know, the two of us in my car, on an empty street, late at night. You remember, back in Kanesville. Only tonight it's not raining. You remember. Don't you?" Her eyes turned up to Charlene's, pleading as if her whole future depended upon Charlene's remembering that long ago night.

Charlene smiled down at her, her arm tightened its embrace, and she answered, "Yes, honey, I remember. I remember very well." Her hand moved, unbuttoned the top of Cynthia's ever-present sweater. Then it slipped inside, cupping and holding and molding the heavy left breast with its prominent nipple. "Now, darling," she said, pulling the girl tighter against her side, "tell me what this is all about, this Karen and Billie thing."

Cynthia looked up at her as if heartened and soothed by Charlene's close presence beside her. She smiled faintly, stirred, brought her hands up and unbuttoned her sweater completely. She gripped the edges and spread the garment wide, and she whispered softly, "All right, Charley darling. I'll tell you everything. But first — " She arched, thrusting her bare breasts forward. "Kiss them, Charley. Please? They've missed you, Charley."

Charlene gazed at the exposed lushness, still amazed at their firmness and thrust. She licked her lips, returned Cynthia's tiny smile, and bent to fulfill the girl's request. Just before her lips closed over one tight nipple her eyes noted that Cynthia's ribs were far more prominent than she had remembered them. Another rush of sympathy mingled with the desire roused by the sweet offerings before her, and when her mouth took possession it did so with a warmth and almost violence that brought a start to Cynthia's whole body. "Charley," she breathed softly.

"Oh Charley, darling . . . " Her hands gripped Charlene's head with spasmodic strength, which was quickly sapped by Charlene's questing mouth. As the strength of her arms weakened, however, the extent of her arch increased, until by the time Charlene drew back from her completely, her breasts were pointed virtually straight up and her breathing and pulse rate were almost frightening in their intensity. Charlene was nearly as shaken as Cynthia, but sh forced herself upright, replaced her arm around the girl's shoulders and her hand on the firm breast.

"Now, Cynthia, I want you to tell me what happened. No more stalling." Cynthia's face lost its glow almost instantly, and she huddled close against Charlene once more.

"Yes," she whispered. "Yes, I guess I can tell you now. Oh Charley, it was awful!" Her voice shook for a moment and she gulped again. "I — I don't know what to do." Her body quaked suddenly, and Charlene held her tightly.

"Damn it, honey, tell me what happened. Then maybe we can decide what to do." Cynthia drew a deep breath. "All right, Charley." She settled herself more snugly against Charlene's side and began a story that, by its horror, put the cap on Charlene's own troubled thoughts.

It began about a week after Charlene's abrupt and unannounced departure from the roadside drive-in where they had first met. Cynthia had obeyed Charlene's suggestion that she avoid the place, until her need to see Charlene had overcome her. She had returned to the drive-in one night, only to see no sign of Charlene. She had gone to Charlene's former living quarters, only to find a "For Rent" sign in front of it. She'd been so shaken by this that she had gone home again without asking any questions of anyone at the drive-in, afraid that she might reveal some sign of her passionate attachment to Charlene. The next night, more in control of herself, she had returned and was sitting in her car debating how to go about asking for information when her car door opened and she watched with shocked eyes as Karen climbed into the seat with her.

Karen was completely casual and friendly, asking off-handedly after Charlene's health. Cynthia had unwittingly let slip the fact that she didn't know what had happened to Charlene, hadn't seen or heard from her since the night . . . well, that night. Karen hard looked Cynthia in silence for a moment, then laughed lightly, saying, "I didn't think so." After another short silence she'd added: "Billie and I have her, you know. We grabbed her a couple of nights ago, and we've got her stashed in a cabin a few miles from here. We decided to teach her a lesson." Another silence. "She's been wanting to see you. She figured you'd be coming back here looking for her, and she asked us if we'd come over and bring you to her."

Karen stopped, looking at Cynthia speculatively, then, seeing that the girl apparently believed her completely thus far, continued: "We figured it couldn't do any harm, so I left Billie in the cabin with Charlene and came over looking for you. She stopped again, looked closely at Cynthia, and winked slowly and suggestively. "Besides, baby, we've got a little unfinished business, remember? You were so eager to protect your little playmate. Now if you were to come with me right now it might take some of our attention off Charlene for a while, make things a lot easier for her." At Cynthia's startled gasp, Karen hastened to reassure her. "Oh, we haven't hurt her — much. She's okay." Another leer followed. "We're teaching her to like us, not hate us." As she said it, the word "like" sounded obscene, and the effect was heightened by a lewd movement of Karen's whole body. Karen, correctly it seemed, interpreted Cynthia's reaction as a surge of jealousy, Karen laughed aloud. "So you see, honey, you can not only get another look at your lover, but you can get us off her back for a while. How about it?"

Cynthia, of course, did not hesitate. "All right," she said. "Get your car, and I'll follow you." Karen, however, waved a hand vaguely toward the darkness outside the light halo cast by the drive-in lights. "Oh, that's all right. I'll pick it up later, when you come back this way. I wouldn't want to take a chance of us losing each other on the road, and the cabin's kinda hard to find at night. I'll ride with you." Five minutes later Karen was warning Cynthia to slow down. "Get us stopped for speeding, and you'll only delay seeing your sweetie."

" — I could turn you into the police, you know. For kidnapping."

Karen laughed. "Honey, by now your Charlene would swear that it was her idea to visit us at the cabin." She paused. "You don't know just how persuasive Billie and I can be. But just you wait till you and I get on with what we started the other night. You liked it then — I could tell — and this time you'll *love* it. I'll see to it." She dropped a hand on Cynthia's thigh and squeezed intimately. "Oh, how you'll love it."

And Karen was right. At the cabin, of course, there was no sign of Charlene, and Cynthia was amazed to see a car pull in behind hers. She was even more amazed to see the stocky Billie get out of it and join her and Karen in front of the cabin door. But before she had time to wonder very much about what was happening she was pushed gently but firmly into the cabin, where with no delay or fussing she was introduced to the persuasive methods of Billie and Karen. Cynthia struggled at first, but the pair was more than she could handle, and they simply laughed at her squirming and protests. In response to her requests to see Charlene right away they impatiently assured her that she ·would see her lover in due time.

Meanwhile, she found herself stripped and stretched out on the bed, while Karen went to work with what seemed to be her favorite implement, a long turkey feather. Cynthia shuddered violently in Charlene's encircling arm as she mentioned the feather, and Charlene felt the breast under her right palm tighten even more, and the nipple hardened — to a big bullet. Charlene gripped tighter, remembering her own experience with that feather, and she knew exactly what Cynthia had gone through.

"Go on, darling," Charlene whispered softly. "Tell me tho rest of it."

Cynthia sobbed once. "I — I can't, Charley. I just can't tell you some of the things I did to them, and let them do to me. *Let them!* Before they were through with me I was begging them to go on. They drove me crazy, Charley. They made me forget about you, even. I couldn't think; I could only feel. When they stopped, finally, I couldn't even feel any more. I was like a zombie. Oh God, Charley . . . " She suddenly broke into another fit of terrible, dry sobs, and Charlene wrapped both arms around the small body, waiting out the storm.

Cynthia composed herself and, her voice growing faint, resumed her story, her face half hidden against Charlene's breast: "Well, I woke up, I don't know how much later, to find myself between them on the bed. Even then, I had to fight myself to try to get up and sneak out of there. I knew, or thought I did, that I wasn't going to see you that night. I was sure they had lied to me about you being there, and I knew I had to get out or go crazy. Anyway, I looked around for my clothes, picked up what I could find and started to ease my way to the door. Then I felt that ungodly feather again, stroking down the length of my back. Charley, I — I couldn't move another step. I was paralyzed. A light came on then, and I heard Karen's voice behind me. 'Tum around here, darling. You're not going to run out on us, are you?' I couldn't help myself, Charley. I turned around, still holding my clothes, and Karen ran the feather down my front, real slow and easy. I dropped the clothes on the floor and just stood there, my knees almost too weak to hold me up. Then Karen dropped the feather and held out her arms. And I went to her, Charley."

"Suddenly I didn't want anything in the world but Karen and Billie and their 'persuasion.' I almost fell into her arms and she half carried me back to the bed. Then it all started over again . . . " Charlene was seething with fury by this time, but it was mixed with remembrance of her own wild passions as they had been aroused by Karen and Billie, and she was abruptly recalled to the present by Cynthia's whispered plea: "Charley, please. You're hurting me." She realized then that her hands had been wandering roughly over Cynthia's nude upper body. She forced her muscles to relax, whispered in return: "I'm sorry, darling. Go on."

"Well," Cynthia continued, "they let me go the next morning. But they made sure I would come back. They apologized for not bringing you to see me, but they'd gotten carried away and forgot all about you; They promised you'd be there the next night."

"On the way home I thought about everything, and I hated them. I hated them worse than anything else I can remember — except myself. I hated myself most of all — but I knew I'd be back that night, whether you were there or not. I knew I couldn't keep away from them, and I hated all three of us more than I could possibly tell you."

"Well, when I got home my parents were frantic with worry. I told them something vague about having car trouble or something, I don't really remember what, and went up to my room. Once I hit the bed I didn't move until almost ten o'clock that night."

"I was almost crazy, Charley. Maybe you were there, and maybe they thought I wasn't coming after all, and maybe they were mad and taking out their spite on you. Then I thought about the night before, and I went even crazier. I had to go, whether you were there or not. I got up and took a quick shower, threw on some clothes and sneaked out, trying not to get my parents' attention. I didn't want to talk to them at all. I couldn't. I drove like a maniac toward that cabin, and I swore all the way because it was such a long drive. And when I got there, it seemed like an anti climax. Karen and Billie were perfectly calm and relaxed, and smiled knowingly at each other when they let me in the door."

"I looked around for you, but Karen laughed at me and told me to relax; they'd bring you in in due time. And then, before I had time to wonder whether they were lying, Karen was after me. She dragged me down on the bed, and in no time I was forgetting about you again"

"All this time Billie was sitting at the table, cutting off slices from a big block of cheese and a carving knife and eating them. Between mouthfuls she was making suggestive remarks and offering advice on Karen's technique with me."

"Well, finally I guess Karen thought I was about ready for any-thing, and she sat on the edge of the bed, stark nude, and hand-ed me two turkey feathers. She made me kneel down between her feet, and then she lay back and told me to — to kiss her and run both of the feathers over her at the same time. You know. She was right. I was ready for anything, so I was only too happy to do what she wanted me to do.

"Well, Karen was twisting and threshing and moaning, and I was so fascinated with trying to please her that I almost didn't hear Billie yell out something like, 'What the hell you want, buster? Gettin' a good eyeful?' Then she laughed; and I turned around to see what had happened. And there outside the window I saw my dad's face. He was staring straight at me, and he had the strang-est, sickest look on his face I've — " Cynthia's voice broke and her face burrowed tighter against Charlene's breast. Charlene spoke sharply. "Cynthia, stop it! It's past and done with. Tell me what happened." She shook the small body, forced the stricken face back and upward. Cynthia's eyes were closed, but she grit-ted her teeth and went on: "Billie was laughing like crazy, while he just went on staring at me through the window. Then I heard Karen laugh behind me. She got up off the bed and went toward the door, swinging herself like a... a *cheap whore*. I guess that must have been what did it. Billie was looking at the window and Karen was just opening the door, both of them still laughing. The knife was lying where Billie had left it on the table and I made a lunge for it. Without even thinking I stuck it clear through Billie's neck from front to back. yanked it out again and caught Karen in the open door. I can remember vaguely seeing my dad running blindly toward the highway, where he must have parted so as not to let us know he had followed me, but I didn't take time to think of that. I swung the bloody knife and rammed it as deep as

I could between Karen's shoulder blades . . . "

Cynthia's voice died away for a moment, then went on with a heartbreaking wistful quality in it "That stopped them laughing." Charlene sat in stunned silence, waiting, but Cynthia seemed to have gone into some private dreamworld of her own. Charlene tangled her fingers in the blonde mop of hair in a protective gesture. "My God," she gasped, "You poor little devil." She cuddled the blonde head, her fingers stroking the hair. "And I thought I had troubles. Go on, baby, finish it." She had to repeat her words three or four times, but finally Cynthia returned from wherever she had been in her nightmare world. When she went on, her voice was calm, but Charlene recognized that calm as the one that signifies thoughts and hopes as dead as Karen and Billie.

"I took my time about dressing," the dead voice continued, "and before I left I checked to see if they were really dead. They were, so far as I could see. I didn't seem to feel any particular way. I just left the cabin and drove home, as if nothing had happened.

"My parents both looked at me with the look I had seen on my father's face, when I walked into the house. I don't know yet whether my father had seen me use the knife on Billie. Maybe he did, maybe not. Anyway, neither of them said anything to me, and I didn't speak to them. I went up to my room and lay down on the bed to think. I knew I had to run. I was a murderer. I knew they'd catch me some time, but I had to run. For the first time in my life that I can remember, I didn't just sink helplessly. I was scared witless, but I was going to run. I got up and packed a bag, got out my bankbook and put it in my purse. Then I lay down again, knowing I couldn't sleep, but hoping that the relaxation of lying down would rest me a little."

"Early the next morning I snuck out of the house again, through the back door. I don't know whether my parents heard me or not. If they did, they showed no sign of it.

"I drove around until the bank opened, went in and drew out my entire savings, and took off. I just went, not caring where, scared to death every time I heard a siren, saw a red light on a car, or came within a block of a police uniform. I wound up in San

Francisco, and that's where I saw the paper with the article about the drive-in you were working in. I haven't seen anything in the papers about Karen and Billie, or about anyone looking for me, but I know they are. And they'll find me eventually. But I'm going to try, Charley. I'm not going to fold up like I always have before. They're going to have to catch me the hard way. I don't feel that I've done anything wrong in killing those two. They deserved it, and I did it, and I'm not a bit sorry. I'm only sorry for my parents, but what good does that do them?

"The only thing I can do is let them forget about me. I hope to God they can. Oh God, what I've done to them . . . " The tone of her last words caused something inside Charlene to curl up and die. She drew Cynthia against her once more, and her tears drenched the blonde hair on the small head cuddled beneath her chin. Her words were scarcely audible, intended more for herself than for Cynthia. "Baby, baby, what I've done to you ... "

The of them huddled together, Charlene no longer the dominant, overpowering individual. She was as lost, and felt as hopeless and helpless, as Cynthia. She knew no more than Cynthia about what they could do, or how to go about it. It never occurred to her to think about herself alone. She had caused Cynthia's troubles, and it was up to her to rack her brain and find a solution. But what solution was there? Neither did it occur to either of them to wonder and marvel at free—flowing tears from Charlene Duval, the all competent and indestructible.

Overhead, unknown to them in the absorption with Cynthia's story, heavy clouds had been gathering, and now, suddenly, there came a slashing downpour, which gradually penetrated their preoccupation with themselves. Cynthia stirred and glanced up at the streaming windshield for a long moment, and her faint smile struggled to assert itself. "Look, Charley," she said, "now it's just like that second night of ours back in Illinois."

Charlene looked, then spoke in a taut voice. "Not quite, honey, not quite. I wish to God it were." She turned to Cynthia. "I've got a story to tell you, too." Cynthia offered no comment, either during or after Charlene's narrative of her experience in California, including the killing of the bartender and her humiliation of

the unknown girl with the Continental. There seemed
nothing to say, under the circumstances, and there was a long,
deep silence between them as they stared at the water streaming down the windshield of the car.

While Charlene was relating her California experiences to Cynthia in the parked car on the long, straight stretch of Nardis
Street, two cursing ambulance men almost mile away were
dashing through the sudden heavy rain toward the vehicle they
had thoughtlessly left parked in the open in front of it ·garage.
"Damn it," groused the driver as he palmed water from his face,
"why can't people get sick or hurt themselves in decent weather,
at least? Where'd that call come from again?"

The other man consulted a slip. "9210 South Nardis. Know
where it is?"

"Yes," groaned the driver. "I know where it is. I know where
everything is. It's about a mile from here, and maybe a half mile
this side of Selmo." He eased out into the street, flashers blinking
and sirens wailing. "I hope these damn fools on the streets aren't
too comfortable and cozy with their closed windows and blasting
radios to hear and see us. I got a thing against dyin' on a night
like this." The siren rose to a scream as they approached an
intersection . . .

In the silence that followed Charlene's narrative both girls tensed
as the wail of an approaching siren came to them through the
drumming of blinding rain on the metal of the car. The siren
shrieked, closer this time, and Cynthia's hand clutched Charlene's knee.

"Charley — Oh God, Charley, what if they've spotted the car?"

"Hush, baby. How could they? No, honey, it's probably a fire engine." Charlene tried a laugh that wasn't too successful. "All this
dry weather, you know ... " But her muscles were quivering with
tension. Cynthia eyed her. "Charley," she said quietly, "start the
engine. I don't want to be caught sitting. We've got to try to get
away, no matter, if it does happen to be them."

Charlene tried another laugh, but her hand went to the key and put the motor into motion. "We'd have a better chance without lights," she remarked. Cynthia said nothing, her head cocked for the next sound of the siren. And when it came, both girls jumped. The damned thing sounded as if it were right behind them, and their eyes automatically went to the rear window. They were just in time to see a red flasher ease around a comer somewhat further back than they would have guessed it to be, and head toward them.

Cynthia whirled, but before she could say a word Charlene was already in motion, and the car, lights out, was moving under far too heavy acceleration for the street conditions.

"Watch for an intersection," Charlene snapped to Cynthia. "Try to give me enough time to get ready for the turn when you see one."

"O—okay, Charley. But please step on it. I won't be caught. I won't!" She almost screamed the words and her fists were white knots against the darkness of her skirt. Her eyes jumped to the mirror again. "Fast er, Charley, they're gaining, I think."

Charlene's foot came down harder on the accelerator, and her eyes squinted to see through the flood left on the windshield in spite of the hard working wipers. "Don't worry, baby," she gritted between clenched teeth. "We'll lose them by winding around through side streets. Nobody but us would be silly enough to drive like this in such a rain. We'll lose them in no time." Her eyes were watering from the strain of trying to see through the windshield, and she blinked and shook her head to clear her vision.

Then, just as she was wondering about a dim glow in the distance and trying to see..what it might be, she was distracted momentarily by Cynthia.'s raised voice.
"Charley! I think we've done it! I can barely see the red light now. They must have given up."
Charlene threw a glance at the mirror, down at the speedometer. My God! Approaching 90! No wonder they had given up. She took her foot off the accelerator as her eyes went back to the street before the careening car.

But it was already too late, even though everything seemed to be in slow motion now Charlene's horrified eyes recognized an overhead light in the middle of the T-intersection, the unmistakable form of a massive concrete wall looming directly ahead and seemingly over them. She felt her body in the grip of complete paralysis, was vaguely grateful that Cynthia was still staring intently out the rear window toward the now invisible red flasher. Even now, however, Charlene was not conscious of the fact that her lips moved, and the voice of a very little girl said: "An' now they're noth —"

· · ·

Back a considerable distance up Nardis Street the two ambulance drivers froze dead still in spite of the pouring rain, shuddering and listening intently for any followup to the hellish sound that had stopped them in mid-stride. Finally, the driver shivered again, and whispered, "That sounds like someone else's problem." Then they went on about their immediate business.

THE END

AND THEN THERE WAS...

WWW.PULPCULTUREPRESS.COM

www.ingramcontent.com/pod-product-compliance
Ingram Content Group UK Ltd.
Pitfield, Milton Keynes, MK11 3LW, UK
UKHW021949040225
4436UKWH00048B/1270